DEBRIS

WITHDRAWN

Markham Public Library
Unionville Branch
15 Library Lane
Unionville, ON L3R 5C4
Feb 2016

DEBRIS
STORIES
KEVIN
HARDCASTLE

A JOHN METCALF BOOK

BIBLIOASIS
Windsor, ON

Copyright © Kevin Hardcastle, 2015

All rights reserved. No part of this publication may be reproduced or transmitted in any form or by any means, electronic or mechanical, including photocopying, recording, or any information storage and retrieval system, without permission in writing from the publisher or a license from The Canadian Copyright Licensing Agency (Access Copyright). For an Access Copyright license visit www.accesscopyright.ca or call toll free to 1-800-893-5777.

FIRST EDITION

Library and Archives Canada Cataloguing in Publication

Hardcastle, Kevin, 1980-, author
       Debris / Kevin Hardcastle.

Short stories.
Issued in print and electronic formats.
ISBN 978-1-77196-040-3 (paperback).--ISBN 978-1-77196-041-0 (ebook)

       I. Title.

PS8615.A68D43 2015   C813'.6   C2015-903742-5
                                             C2015-903743-3

Canada Council   Conseil des Arts   Canadian   Patrimoine
for the Arts   du Canada   Heritage   canadien

ONTARIO ARTS COUNCIL
CONSEIL DES ARTS DE L'ONTARIO
50 YEARS OF ONTARIO GOVERNMENT SUPPORT OF THE ARTS
50 ANS DE SOUTIEN DU GOUVERNEMENT DE L'ONTARIO AUX ARTS

Biblioasis acknowledges the ongoing financial support of the Government of Canada through the Canada Council for the Arts, Canadian Heritage, the Canada Book Fund; and the Government of Ontario through the Ontario Arts Council and the Ontario Media Development Corporation.

Edited by John Metcalf
Copy-edited by Allana Amlin
Typeset and designed by Kate Hargreaves
Cover image by angelandspot

PRINTED AND BOUND IN CANADA

MIX
Paper from
responsible sources
FSC® C004071
www.fsc.org

ANCIENT FOREST ™
FRIENDLY

CONTENTS

OLD MAN MARCHUK

TWO NARROW BEAMS OF HALOGEN light crisscrossed over the black prairie, found the warped and weathered sideboards of old man Marchuk's barn. An eerie blue round settled over the chained and padlocked barndoor handles. Up into the light rose a three-foot boltcutter. One man held the flashlight steady. One man slid the cutter-blades over the padlock shackle and squeezed hard on either handle. He had to reset twice before he'd cut through. The man with the light fussed with the lock until he freed it and could pull the chains clear. Then he pocketed the flashlight in his coveralls while he dragged the great barn doors open, his face lit like a jack-o'-lantern.

The cutter man had gotten to their one-ton pickup and he was backing it over toward the barnmouth, pushing a tow trailer by the hitch. He stopped short enough for the other man to loose and unfold the ramp to the trailer. The man in the truck waited while his partner hotwired a pair of four-wheelers and drove the first up the ramp onto the trailer bed, engine growling high. He parked it and went back for the other. Drove it into place and shut the engine off. The driver of the truck drummed the window frame and watched, red cherry of his smoke glowing in the black. The other man raised the trailer ramp and fixed it shut. He started for the passenger side of the truck and froze three steps out.

They'd not heard the squelching of bootfalls in the thawmud near the barn. Not until the old man was right on top of them with his twelve-gauge raised high, stock pinned against his shoulder. Marchuk pulled and sprayed the driver's door. Muzzlefire showed him briefly against the outer blackness. The driver barked like a dog, ducked low and tried to cover up. Marchuk took aim again. The young man at the rear of the truck pitched his flashlight and it flew end over end past old man Marchuk's wild-haired head. Marchuk spun and fired blindly at the spot. The young man dropped to the muck and shrieked. He'd taken shot in the side and through his upper leg but he managed to clamber onto the trailer and fall in behind the last four-wheeler just as his buddy punched the gas and sent the truck tires spinning. The old man had shucked his spent shells and set about reloading. Marchuk emptied both barrels on the truck and its trailer as the vehicle sped off serpentine through his fenceless backfields.

He came upon the trailered vehicle not ten miles down the county road. The driver sped just slightly and held the road straight. Marchuk drove an old Dodge pickup and he had his running lights turned off. He drifted up alongside the larger truck until he could see both men sitting wounded in the cab. When the driver turned and saw the old man coasting along beside him he panicked and swerved wide, caught the edge of the roadside drainage ditch and pulled back. The trailer nearly jackknifed before skittering back in line on the weather-buckled asphalt. Old man Marchuk cut into the other lane and the driver of the one-ton chickened out and slammed his brakes, went too far wide this time and ended up ploughing sandied ditchturf for about a hundred feet before the vehicle shuddered to a stop. Marchuk got out with the scattergun and pumped holes through the driver door.

CONSTABLE TOM HOYE GOT THE CALL from dispatch and had to floor it from two townships over. He saw four red eyes in the road and then felt a series of little thuds on the car's undercarriage. He drove on. The constable had lately been stationed at the lonely RCMP detachment that served the county, with its three-man rotation and one dispatch to cover four barren townships. They got calls of gunfire a few times a week and heard gunfire every night. That night was the first they'd gotten a call from the man who actually fired the shots, and that man went by the name of Marchuk. Hoye took the details as he drove.

"What's he sayin' he shot at?" Hoye said.

"Two men tryin' to steal his ATVs," said the girl at dispatch. "But he's not sayin' he shot at them. He's sayin' he shot them."

"What?"

"How far out are you?"

"Seven or eight minutes. Where's the EMT?"

"They won't be a minute behind you if at all."

WHEN CONSTABLE HOYE PULLED UP to the scene he saw the one-ton tipped over in the ditch, shards of windowglass that shone by the light of the cruiser's headlamps. Marchuk was leaning up against the side of his own truck, one foot crossed over the other, cradling his shotgun in the crook of his arm. The old man put one hand up against the headlights. Constable Hoye got out of the car with his hand on his pistol. He flicked the safety off as he stood. Marchuk just waited there, taking the air as the constable came over. Plains wind travelled warm and gentle through the pass. The faint sound of ambulance sirens called out from afar.

"Set your firearm down on the ground and step away," Hoye said.

Marchuk frowned at him. Hoye had to pull his pistol and let it hang before the old man knelt and laid the weapon down on the tarmac. The constable waited until Marchuk stepped clear and then he gestured for him to keep going.

"Put your hands on the hood of your truck," he said.

"Son, you are wastin' my time," the old man said.

"Put your fuckin' hands on the hood I said. And stay put."

Marchuk sauntered over and did it, slapping his palms down like a showy child. He stood there in his coveralls. Sandpaper beard and huge, crooked nose. Hoye passed him and stepped down into the ditch. Took his flashlight out of his belt and turned it on. When he shone the beam over the ditchhill he saw pieces of the truck's upholstery scattered across the turf like cottongrass, a full section of door siding with thin furrows in the mold. Then he saw the two shot men. One was on his side in the ditchbasin, his legs shuffling. The other lay starfished against the hillside in his bandit-blacks and he didn't move at all.

"Jesus fuckin' Christ," Hoye said.

He started to go for the men and then he stopped and levelled his pistol at Marchuk. The old man took his hands off the hood and put them up until Hoye barked at him to put them back. The constable came back into the road and took out his cuffs and braceletted the old man's bony wrists.

"Just what the fuck are ye doin', son?" said Marchuk.

"You shot those men?"

"They were robbin' me."

"Your farm is fuckin' three miles thataway," Hoye said, nodding south.

The old man stared at him sourfaced. The back of his scraggly head lit up in colours. An EMT wagon crested a rise in the roadway and coasted toward them. Hoye stepped out into the lane and waved it down.

HE CAME HOME AN HOUR BEFORE sunrise, the sky paling to the east. The constable and his wife had rented a two-storey brownstone with no house number. Just their name stencilled on the mailbox. Their nearest neighbour was a gravel quarry some three miles away. Hoye parked the cruiser in the driveway and went into the house through the sideporch entrance. He hung his keys and undressed, put his jacket and his Kevlar over the back of a wooden dining table chair. Laid his pants overtop, flat to the crease. Then he went to the fridge and knuckled up two bottles of beer. He sat on the living room couch with the TV on but nearly inaudible. The bottles were empty after maybe five pulls so he got up to grab another.

Hoye's eyes had turned to slits when the stairwell groaned behind him. He stood up and saw his wife descending slowly, tiny bubble of tongue bit between her lips as she concentrated on landing each footfall. She followed a dogleg near the stair-bottom and made her way down the last three steps. The young woman stood maybe five-foot-three with copper hair and a round, round belly pushing up the cloth of her nightie.

"Hey," she said. "Nice outfit."

Hoye stood there in his gitch, his blues unbuttoned and his undershirt showing. He had the legs of a quarterhorse.

"What time is it, Jenny?" he said.

"It's not morning and it's not night," she said.

He watched her shuffle past the couch and she eyed him sidelong as she went. She started smiling, deep dimple at her right cheek.

"If you sneezed I think you might pop," he said.

"Are you gonna go to bed or what?" she said.

"I didn't really think that far ahead."

"What happened out there?"

"That old fella Marchuk pumped about six rounds of buckshot into two city boys who were stealin' his ATVs."

"My God," she said. "Are they alive?"

He nodded.

"Somehow."

"How was he when you took him?"

"He didn't think he did nothing wrong."

She went into the kitchen and he heard the cupboards opening and closing. He came in to help her but she shooed him. Hoye got behind his wife and put his arms around her shoulders, held the belly in his big hands, his chin pinned to her shoulderblade. She reached up and cupped his cheek.

"Get off me you big oaf," she said, but she didn't move. Finally he kissed her neck and stood up tall, let her loose.

"Go to bed for a couple hours," Jenny said. "I'm not going anywhere."

So he did.

THE TWO YOUNG BURGLARS DIDN'T DIE but came about as close to it as they could. The driver lost one of his feet and the meat of his right triceps and he had nerve damage throughout. The other burglar flatlined three times during surgery and that was after he'd almost bled out in the ambulance. They were under police guard and would be until they were fit for trial. But not their trial. They had pled guilty by proxy and were sentenced to community service and probation.

The trial they awaited was Marchuk's. The old man had been arraigned and pled not guilty before cussing out the court and the sitting judge.

The old man had lands and money enough to post his bail-bond, high as it was, but some folks from that township and those that bordered some-how anted up the cost and posted for him. On a pretty autumn day Marchuk left the stationhouse shaking his head and then he drove back to his farm in his old Dodge. There he took back the tending of his property from cousins who had driven in from north-interior British Columbia. They didn't go back. Instead they shacked up with him and awaited the trial.

THE FIRST ATTACK AGAINST HOYE WAS no more than the rude spray painting of the words "Eastern Pig" on his garage door. He managed to acetone the graffiti clear before his wife got a chance to see it. Hoye heard rumblings of who might have done it and he let it be known that the drinking age in that county was about to be enforced nightly. Fines to be given out and liquor to be confiscated. Two weeks later somebody tore up the sideyard of his house by spinning doughnuts all over the crabgrassed turf. It happened when he was out on patrol and when he got home he found Jenny on the porch steps with a pump shotgun on her lap. Shells in a line on the wooden planking beside her. He had to talk a long time before he could get his gun back. They went inside and sat together in the kitchen.

"What, are they retarded or something?" she said.

"They just ain't accustomed to having someone tell them no. But they're gonna figure it out real quick."

Jenny sipped at a glass of water, the fingers of her right hand lightly stained with gun grease.

"He nearly killed those kids."

"They think it was justified."

"We don't live in Texas."

"If we did he'd still be locked up. They would've had to be inside his house for him to open fire."

"How much longer do we have before you can pick a new station?"

"One year, three months, and eighteen days."

Jenny stood up slowly. Took up his empty beer bottle and carried it over to the counter. She got him another from the fridge and set it down.

"I just hope they quit it."

Hoye pulled hard on the bottle, set it down on the kitchen table and stared at it. At the rough hand holding it.

"They will," he said.

JENNY HOYE DROVE OVER AN HOUR TO get to the nearest big-box store. She took trips there weekly to load up on diapers and formula, toiletries, other household necessaries. From those narrow, sunbaked roads she saw miles and miles of shortgrassed dunes, low-rolling plains with not a pond or trickle of river. Rare sightings of stunted trees with their barks dried and sloughing. Remains of groundhogs and coyotes on the macadam or otherwise strewn in the roadside gravel. Once in a while a lonely oilfield pumpjack with its counterweight turning anticlockwise and its steel horsehead dipping low and rising again. There was a base and barracks in the town and on her visits she would see men in army camos trailing their wives down the aisles, some upright and solemn and others leaning down heavy to the carthandles as they shoved along.

She filled her cart and pushed it to the checkout line. When she rung through a young stockboy with a harelip asked her if she needed a hand getting out. Jenny told him thanks but she'd be okay. He smiled shyly and went on. She wheeled the cart out into the lot and found her parking spot. As she was loading the trunk she heard someone calling her name. Jenny turned to see a young woman hailing her from across the lot.

"Fuck," she said.

ON THE WAY HOME SHE SAW a four-door pickup in her rear-view mirror and it stayed there. Monster tires and a heavy steel grillguard. Mud and muck on the hood and windshield. Jenny drove through town and took a turn that she didn't need to take and the truck kept on straight. She snaked home through the county roads and there on the last length of dirt lane the jacked-up truck stood idling at an intersection, not a half-mile from her house. It pulled into the lane behind her and followed close. She could see sunburnt forearms hanging thick on either side of the vehicle. There were at least four men, two in front and the rest in back. She nearly drove on past the house but cut a hard right at the last second and skittered onto the gravel driveway. The truck slowed but kept on. Four sets of eyes on the woman as she got out and studied the vehicle and the muddied British Columbia plates. A gun rack had been fixed in the back window of the truck and all the brackets were full.

HOYE PULLED INTO THE FARM'S FRONTLOT at dusk with two cruisers trailing him. He saw lamp-light through the thin-curtained upper windows. Brighter lights in the kitchen. The sound of country music and raised voices travelling raucous from an open side door. There was no proper driveway, just a ruined patch of land in front of the house filled with vehicles. Battered pickups and rusted-out car frames on blocks and a gargantuan RV parked sidelong to the house, power cables running between the two like tentacles. A raised, extended-cab pickup with B.C. plates. Hoye pulled in first and the other cars fol-lowed. Each cruiser rode two officers and they got out armed and armoured and Hoye took two of them toward that kitchen side-entry. Hoye was certain that there would be dogs to give them away early, but there were not.

When they walked in through the kitchen screen door it squealed on its springs. Four men sat at a massive oak-slab table with bottles of beer and whis-key staining the lumber. Two women were tending the stove. One middle-aged and greying, stout and square-jawed. The other young and dirty blonde and very pretty, a scattering of old pox-scars on her cheek and forehead. Hoye and his two constables came into the room and spread out, eyeballed the foreign men, hands on the heels of their pistols. A door shut somewhere in the back of the house and soon enough the three other constables filled the doorway at the other side of the kitchen. Hoye knocked a stack of papers from a nearby chair where it sat below a wall-mounted rotary phone. He spun the chair to the table and sat. Across from him sat old man Marchuk and he tried to stare a hole through Hoye. Black, biblical hate in his eyes. Hoye just stared back.

"You know that there's warrants out for your cousins here, from B.C., and they're to be escorted to the border and placed in custody there."

"That is a load of horseshit," Marchuk said. "What for?"

"I've got 'Fight Causing a Disturbance' for a Bretton Marchuk and 'Cultivation of Marijuana' for Gary Myshaniuk and Mark Oulette. The rest can just go in for assisting wanted fugitives."

"They're my guests and they aren't goin' anywheres. So you can go fuck yourself. You ain't got no warrant or cause to come into my house."

"We don't need a warrant to seize the wanted men. But I'll be kind and give them a chance to drive their asses outta here to the border under escort. Or they could get shot instead in this fuckin' kitchen for all I care. Seems to be a way of life for you folks."

Marchuk tried to get out of his chair and Hoye stood and sat him back down by the shoulder.

OLD MAN MARCHUK WAS TAKEN into custody and locked up in the station holding cell while his cousins were driven west, handed off from detachment to detachment until they were released to officers from Golden. Bretton Marchuk had a broken nose plugged with bloody tissue when he was put under arrest inside British Columbia. The other men were marked with facial lacerations and contusions along their forearm and shinbones. The elder woman, wife to the cousin Marchuk, spat at one of the B.C. constables and then watched her husband take a baton to both of his knees. She held her spit from then on. The constables released the younger, blonde woman alone, and let her take the truck back to their lands in the foothills.

Marchuk saw his bail rescinded and spent his days and nights in holding at the Red Deer Remand Centre. He got letters and visits from townsfolk. Few people would speak to Hoye or his wife, any of the other officers or their families, even those born in that township. Hoye did not mind. One day he found their lawn staked with dozens of "For Sale" signs. He pulled them and stacked them in the garage.

ON SHIFT NEAR DAYSLAND, CONSTABLE Hoye had his radio flare up and the dispatch told him that his wife had been taken by ambulance to the hospital in Red Deer. Jenny Hoye had gone into labour nearly a full month early. The constable lit his sirens and drove those black nightroads with the gas pedal pinned. He pulled into the hospital lot just before midnight and found triage, took directions to the labour and delivery rooms.

Hoye wore scrubs over his uniform and they let him into delivery. Jenny gripped his hand hard. Her hair had gone dark with sweat and stuck to her forehead. She had taken no epidural and had just begun to crown. Hoye bent to better see her face. He wiped her brow with a wetcloth and tried to get the hair from her eyes.

"It's alright, Jenny," he said.

"Oh, fuck this," she said.

The doctors had her breathe and push. She hollered and swore and gritted her teeth. Again and again until the baby's shoulders cleared. The boy was born blue with the umbilical wound tight around his neck and upper arm. The doctors went to work unwinding the cord. Jenny had gone pale and stared at the little shut eyelids and the soft skin of his discoloured arms. Blood and mucous on her gown and at her inner thighs. Constable Hoye could barely stand and he waited cold by the hospital bed. It took four minutes for the baby to breathe and when he did he spoke in a wail and reached out with his tiny arms, cycled his feet in the air.

THE CONSTABLE WATCHED HIS WIFE and son through the night and spoke to the attending doctors. The boy had no ill effects from the tangled cord and he'd been born heavy for a premature baby, had a strong heart and lungs to cry with. Hoye left in the morning and he hadn't slept at all. He went to the house with a list and gathered things for his wife. He stood over the patch of kitchen floor where Jenny had been when her water broke. He didn't know whether to clean it or not. After passing it by a few times on his rounds Hoye filled a bucket with soapy water and bleach and started mopping the tile.

Jenny stayed with the baby in the maternal and newborn unit of the hospital for the better part of two weeks. Constable Hoye came every day between shifts or he had another constable cover while he left his watch for an hour or two. He spoke to his son in whispers while Jenny slept.

THE MARCHUK TRIAL HAD BEEN SET FOR A neutral, closed court in Calgary. It started on a Tuesday morning and did not look like it would last a week, so shoddy was the defense. Hoye gave testimony on the third day of the trial and when he came home he found his mailbox rent apart, pebbles of buckshot rattling around inside the deformed container when he pried it clear from the post. He flung it into the garage and drove to the hardware store in town.

The clerk limped slightly as he took Hoye down the shelf rows. A tall man of nearly seventy with a white moustache and short-cropped hair. He had no glasses but seemed to need some more than a little. He showed Hoye toward the mailboxes, most of them antiquated and covered in light dust. Hoye picked out the plainest one and followed the old man toward the buckets of screws and fasteners.

"Heard you had a boy," the man said.

"We did."

The clerk offered his hand. Hoye took it. Hoye was of the same height and wider by a foot but the old man's hand outsized his by far.

"You gonna raise him here?"

"Likely not," Hoye said.

The clerk smiled a little and stood with his knuckles to his hips, picked a stray bolt from a bin and put it back where it belonged. They started back toward the register. Hoye held up.

"Hang on a minute," he said.

Hoye went back to where he'd been shown the mailboxes and he came back to the counter with a second. The clerk had set the first on the woodtop beside the till. Hoye handed him the other and the man nodded and started to tally it all. He found a cardboard box behind the counter and filled it with the goods. Hoye paid him in cash.

"I suppose I don't have to tell you to be careful out there," the clerk said.

"No. But I appreciate it."

"It's not the whole town that's sided against you, young man, or even the half of it. But those that have are awful loud. If you know what I mean."

Hoye nodded and shook the clerk's hand again.

"If you run through those two just come back and I'll get you another, on the house."

Hoye laughed. Waved at the clerk as he went out the door. Wind chimes jangled where they hung from the lintel.

ON A DRY AND SUN-BLEACHED afternoon Constable Hoye pulled up to his homestead with his wife and newborn son. He'd been given a week's worth of leave. A cruiser waited at the roadside near the house. Hoye stopped to say hello and the constable in the other cruiser made faces at the baby in the back seat, the little boy in a safety chair beside his mother. The other constable shook Hoye's hand.

"How're you all handling it?" Hoye said.

"They got a fella from up near Viking that makes his rounds a little further south. He don't seem to mind. Shifts go long they're givin' us OT."

"Well, thank 'em for me will ya?"

"Sure," the constable said. "Keep your radio nearby. Anything comes up I'll squawk at ya."

Hoye nodded and drove on, turned onto the width of gravel in front of the house. The cruiser crept out and took off down the county road. Hoye parked and came around the car to help Jenny. He wore her many bags and bundles on his arms like he were a clothes maiden. Jenny took the boy up in her arms and swaddled him to her chest and neck. She turned him slow so that he could stare out goggle-eyed at the fields and fencewires and hovering birds.

"We get a new mailbox?" she said.

Hoye stood there with the bags dangling. He nodded.

"Old one sort of blew in. So I got another, pegged it down a little sturdier."

Jenny studied the box some more and then she kissed the baby on his pale and peach-fuzzed head and went down the walk to the house. Hoye kicked the car door shut with the toe of his shoe.

HOYE LAY IN THE BED UNTIL THEY both slept. When he got up he went quiet as he could, clicking sound in his knees and his left ankle joint. He turned at the door and saw the dent in the mattress where he rested his bones of a night, his tiny son but inches from it, curled up and pinned to his wife. It hurt his heart just to look at her there, wild-haired as she was in sleep, snoring lightly, so much bigger than their boy. It flooded hollows in him. Cold travelled along his spine and shortribs. He didn't want to leave but he did. He'd found cargo shorts in the laundry hamper and put them on, along with a clean undershirt. He went through the dark house and he knew it less by touch than he should have.

*

OUT ON THE DRIVEWAY HE SAT, garage door open to a tiny nightlight and a fridge of cold beer. Crickets had gotten into the garage and they trilled from their hiding spots. He had an old poker table set up with cans of beer in every cup holder, a bottle of Irish whiskey standing quarter-empty on the felt. The Remington pump lay on a wooden crate beside his chair, five cartridges in the magazine. Chinook wind blew warm across the prairie, slowly spun a crooked weathervane that had been long ago fixed atop the high front gable of the house. Hoye had his Kevlar on over his cottons and the shirtcloth clung to his stomach and lower back. He heard distant reports of rifle-fire. High whine of small engines. Coyotes whooping at each other in a nearby field. Hoye sat there and watched either end of the long, country road. His portable CB radio sat on the table, silent except for sparse chatter between the dispatch and the constables as they roamed the territories.

THE ROPE

HE TOOK THE CAR OVER buckled macadam and followed the forest lane until it was just clay and crabgrass. Sunlight got stuck in the treecover and played weird shapes through the windshield. Soon Matthew hit a clearing and across it sat the log bungalow with thin smoke spiralling heavenward by a metal chimney pipe. He crossed to a gravel lot and just sort of stopped crooked in the middle of it, called that his parking job and got out and stretched his lower back. He left the door open with his things on the seats and walked the clearing to the house.

She was out cold on the big chesterfield with her legs bent up and her hands pegged together between her knees. She snored soft and her left eye stayed open a little bit and stared blind to God knows where. Matthew crossed the cabin room. Clean as could be.

Ghost of a bleaching not long past and it scented the air. Bookshelves and shelves of knickknacks all organized and orderly. He went into the kitchen and looked inside the fridge. Tupperware containers of food and very little of it. Orange juice. Meal replacement sludge. Cheeses and butter. He took up the juice and drank from the container, kept watch on her while he did.

He went over and put a blanket over his mother. He lowered it gentle, his one knee to the hardwood. There he leaned in close and inhaled by her part-open mouth. Stale beer in her breath. Matthew looked over his shoulder to the southernmost wall of the place. By the clock it was eleven twenty-one in the morning.

THE MOON RIVER RAN SLOW PAST the cabin grounds, sparely fished by anyone. Matthew had untethered the cords that held tarpaulin to an old canoe rack aside the little house. He'd beat the canoe clear for spiders and snakes with an old broom and hauled it down to a sandied flat where he could launch it, three-foot-high rockshelves on either side. He left the bank with a huge wooden oar and a fishing rod he'd not touched in decades. The current helped him shuck the beachmud and carry out.

WHEN HE GOT BACK TO THE HOUSE she'd woke and he could find none of his bags. They were stowed in the closet and his shirts and pants hung in with hers. He'd brought a bag of dirty clothes and they were gone. As he walked the place to the cellar stairs he could hear laundry being run and the washing machine rattling down there on its moorings. Maryanna met him on the stairs and turned him and he went back up into the kitchen.

"I was gonna do that," he said.

"I've done it now," she said.

She came up the stairs slow and he didn't like her bringing up the rear with her back to the wood steps and the dark and the concrete.

AT MORNING SHE GOT HIM TO STIR by turning the radio on. Matthew lay deep in a mattress pulled out of the living room chesterfield. He'd slept in his shorts and his T-shirt and usually he didn't sleep like that. Maryanna had been up for some time without waking him. The little house smelled like bacon grease but he couldn't hear it frying.

"I don't know that I'll have time for that," Matthew said.

Maryanna started taking plates out of the oven. Then she lay his breakfast on the table. He came over with his hair stuck out to the side and sat down to eat.

THEY SAT OUTSIDE THE COURTROOM with the townies and skids and some suited men who might have been counsel and might have been clients. When Matthew was in grade school that was a civic centre where he'd play pool and watch horror movies come Halloween with the youth workers that ran it. The waiting area had rows of blue, plastic chairs and side offices where duty counsel sat with those to be heard in the court. Cinder block walls painted pale. They'd settled by eight forty-five in the morning and saw a duty counsellor within the hour.

It was near two in the afternoon when the impaired driving charges were read aloud and plead to by Maryanna. She had a petition from her shrink to say that she suffered depression and anxiety and had some signs of psychosis. The shrink had put her ass on the line with that letter and asked for the charges to be made non-criminal, but there was nothing to be done. Maryanna took the weight of it but the judge at least didn't lecture her nor scold her for what she'd done. Still, he levied the fines. He had a round head and a neat, white beard and the look of a man who never slept. On the way out of the courtroom Maryanna handed the paperwork to Matthew and he carried it, loosed and pulled his tie clear before they'd left the building.

SHE GOT UNDRESSED WITH THE DOOR open and it didn't seem to bother her. When she had her regular clothes on she came back through the house and sat at the kitchen table. She smoked there at the little table and Matthew sat across from her in his dress pants and undershirt.

"Okay, ma?" he said.

Maryanna nodded and smiled funny.

"How d'you feel now?"

"Not very good. Not very good at all."

Matthew studied her long and he felt like getting up and walking the room but he didn't.

"You been havin' bad thoughts?"

"Sometimes."

"Like what kind?"

"It's the stress of it all."

She stubbed out and sat back with her hands in her lap.

"You don't got a plan, do you?" Matthew said.

"I've got a rope."

"Where?"

"In the bedroom drawer."

Matthew stayed still but his heart beat way up in his ears. He took heavy breaths and it was hard for him to keep them in check for he'd a bone-broken nose that let air in poorly by the one nostril.

Maryanna reached over and took his hand in the both of hers. She seemed to have woke up all of a sudden and she scooted her chair in close to him.

"Don't worry about me," she said. "I'm not gonna do that."

THEY WENT TWO TOWNS OVER WHERE the shrink kept an office. Past foundered barns and creeks dried to runnels and mile upon mile of wire fencework. There were fields with showhorses in them, blankets over their backs. Matthew's mother frowned.

"You don't like the horses?" he said.

"I like them fine," she said. "But this is just stupid."

The shrink's office held the main floor of an old Victorian house outside of the town proper. When they pulled in and got out of the car there were banker's boxes stacked on the porch. Matthew followed his mother up the steps and lifted one of the lids as he passed. Full with documents and file folders.

"She ain't wastin' any time gettin' retired," Matthew said.

His mother didn't say anything and she didn't turn.

HE STAYED ON ANOTHER DAY AND then left her with a stocked fridge and crates of non-alcoholic beer. He'd brought her book upon book and new movies and tubes of acrylics as she used to like painting and still had her easel and some canvasses. The keys for her truck were hung on a pegboard near the front door and he took them off. Matthew thought about taking them with him, but instead he hid them in a clay jar and slid that jar deep into a high cupboard. Front and centre on the fridge were the emergency contacts for the retiring shrink. Her personal mobile number. There were no contacts for her replacement because there wasn't one yet and no word on when there would be.

A week later Matthew came back to the house and the clearing was thick with leaves. Bright reds and yellows in with those begun to rot. It looked awful pretty. The sun shone hot from the west but there were great fir columns around the property and they threw shade. When Matthew pulled into the lot he could see her truck under its covers, bricks set on the hood and the roof to pin them down. He started for the house with his bags and then he stopped and set them down in the gravel. He went over to the covered truck and stood beside it and stared at it awhile. Not one leaf lay on those vinyls.

"YOU UNDERSTAND WHY YOU can't drive no more, right?"

She'd not acknowledge him. She kept running lines in the kitchen floor with a dust mop. Matthew watched her move slow and use the mophandle to steady herself. She pushed on.

"What d'you expect me to do, son? Just sit out here an' rot?"

"I'm up here now for the month at work. The Bala site. I'm gonna stay here with ya."

Maryanna stopped moving the mop and set it by against the counter. She seemed to be thinking on it and thinking on it. After a minute she came over to him and put her arms around his neck. He could feel her shoulderblades through the cloth of her shirt. She let him go and went back to the cleaning.

"You just stay busy here and I'll take you where you gotta go when I get home of a night."

"Okay."

"You won't drive that truck?"

"I won't."

"Good," he said. "They pinch you for that again, they'll bury you under the goddamn jail."

HE CAME HOME EVENINGS and sometimes she had already gone to bed. Often she would be there cooking and she'd put his dinner on the table and eat some of her own, move the rest around the plate. For days Maryanna would be fine and then she just wouldn't be. Matthew found clothes in the laundry with piss through them and once she'd soiled her pants and more than once he found blood dried maroon in the cloth. Weight came off her day by day.

Partway through his third week Matthew left the job site early and hustled back to the cabin. He couldn't find her and he couldn't find her. The truck wasn't moved nor had it been in days. He happened upon her in the woodshed and she was downing beer that she'd hidden in with the stacked cords. He started to give her shit for it and she watched him goggle-eyed and he couldn't go through with it. Later he put her to bed with the sun bright behind her bedroom shades and there she shuffled in the blankets and eventually snored.

He trekked the grounds and the near woods before sundown. She'd caches of beer all around the place. By the river he found a hollow where she'd sunk empty bottles and they stood underwater in the mud. He came back with a bag and pulled them one by one. A bottle that he raised had a minnow circling inside. He watched it awhile through the brown glass and then he tipped the bottle and bagged it.

MARYANNA WOULDN'T GET OUT OF HER bed for more than a few hours at a time. She slept odd and the meds put her deep under. Matthew called the shrink's emergency number over and over and he left messages. He stared holes in the sheet and the shrink's handwriting while washing the dishes and sweeping dust and leaf particles out of the cabin. He took a rusted, riding mower over the clearing to mulch the detritus and ended up wearing most of it. When he tried to clean the little bathroom and the toilet he couldn't get it all the way clean as it usually was and that puzzled him.

THE COUNTY HOSPITAL ADMITTED Maryanna and found her a bed. Her ferritin levels were at three thousand and she had welts on her forearms. Maryanna stayed the night under observation and shared a room with a lady of seventy who had a shattered hip. When Matthew picked her up the next day Maryanna had the other lady in the room laughing. She introduced him to the roommate.

"This is my boy," Maryanna said. "He's the one who looks after me."

Matthew shook the old lady's hand. He held it gentle but she had metal bones and squeezed hard enough that his palm hurt. He smiled.

By the weekend Maryanna had cleaned out and came around. She got up early and redid all of the things he'd tried around the house. Matthew ate a pile of breakfast and Maryanna ate well enough and she drank a lot of coffee.

"Shall we go to town today?" she said.

"How d'you feel?"

"I feel like we should go to town."

She took his plates to the sink and Matthew waited a second and then he snagged her purse from where it sat on the near chair and found her wallet. He held it in his lap and got his own wallet out of the rear pocket of his jeans. Matthew looked at her back and waited a second. He pulled her bankcard from his wallet and slid it back into hers.

HE STOOD RIGHT IN FRONT OF THE CABIN and poured an entire two-litre bottle of cider out into the bracken. Sickly smell of it as it went and some of the stuff got on the toe of his shoe and wet his sock. Maryanna watched him blankly and he'd rather have seen her spitting mad and breaking furniture.

"I suppose you think that's funny," she said.

"I fucking well don't," Matthew said.

She went inside and he sat out a long time and he was scared to go back into the house. Eventually he started to shake in his T-shirt with a westerly blowing cool across the near waters. He got up and went in through the screen door and there she was sitting plumb in the kitchen floor with another bottle upended to her mouth. Maryanna stood the cider bottle on the tile and there were but inches left in the bottom. She held the neck between her thumb and forefinger and danced the plastic around the flooring. Drank again. Matthew took his keys and left out.

SHE WAS ON THE CHESTERFIELD again while he pulled bottles from the two beer crates and lined the fridge with them. He moved the milk jugs and plastics to the sink to better fit all the bottles. He went through the living room and put the TV on loud enough that she stirred and settled again. Then he sat at the kitchen table and started downing beers.

By midnight they were both of them polluted and when Matthew spoke he hollered. Maryanna put tapes into an old stereo and played them and they were Maryanna and her sister singing some thirty years before. Warbling of the worn tape-reels that made them sound underwater every few seconds. She played it until she cried and then Matthew got up and turned the tapes off and he wouldn't listen anymore. The boy and his mother talked long at the table and Matthew thumped his beers until they sat high in his chest and then he started to lurch. He went outside and in opening the cabin door he tore the screen loose and kept on. He puked foam and cold beer on the grass fringe near the front steps and he did it as he walked.

An hour later his shirt was in the sink in a ball and he sat there angry and blind with his chest bare and the many burns and blued scars plainly visible. Most of them nearly old as he was. Maryanna had a likewise ugly scar high on her shoulder and it had been a deep cut and uneven and had a valley to it. She tried to get Matthew out of the chair but he would not go. He drank another beer and another and he would not go whatever she said to him.

HE SAT UP DESTROYED IN THE thin morning and he was on the chesterfield mattress where she had dragged him. Where she had dragged him. It didn't make any more sense than if she'd set the two hundred and ten pounds of him on the moon. Matthew dropped back to the pillows again and closed his eyes. He woke again and his mother was sitting in the bed with him. Maryanna had her hand in his hair and the pads of her fingers travelled overtop his ear. She'd cleaned up and tied her hair back and she wore a dress that he'd not seen in years. She held out a glass of water and he sat up full to drink it.

MATTHEW WAS THERE AT THE CABIN when the mechanics came to install the interlock device on

Maryanna's truck. She'd not put a drink to her lips in three months and her impaired fines were paid. The technician worked in the cab of the truck, the temperature just above freezing. There were yet no snows come to the river valley or the towns around it and Christmas had passed with little more than morning frost in the grass and leafless trees with squirrels standing baffled on the branches.

They drove to town together and Maryanna had the wheel. She'd put ten pounds back into her arms and legs and face, and her cheeks held some colour. Her hands had their little tremors and she smoked too much on the drive. No matter. The truck ran well and she drove too fast but Matthew didn't mind. They passed vast acres of cranberry swamp and Maryanna pointed out bear scat on the gravel fringe where it shouldn't have been.

SHE DID NOT USE THE ROPE. Instead she nearly froze to death in the cab of her truck. Dressed in her nightgown and a thin coat and her snow boots. The interlock popped three times and shut the engine down and there Maryanna lay down on the benchseat and didn't get back up. She had frostbitten skin and her eyes closed and a blood-alcohol level that spoke to a life's work. A passing snowmobiler saw hazards and headlights flashing through the wood. Found her locked in the vehicle and called the cops out to the site. They couldn't get an ambulance down the winding trail and the cops had to carry Maryanna out of there in the bed of their suv, her body wrapped in blankets, slow through the pass until they could hand her off to the paramedics.

At the hospital she would not give it up. They treated her for hypothermia and pumped her stomach and she kept losing consciousness and coming back and she couldn't talk at all. When Matthew got there he was beside himself and he couldn't find a doctor. Eventually the doctor showed and Matthew heard him out and then lit into him. The cops tried to make Matthew go home.

"You ever shot a man 'cause he wouldn't leave the hospital?" Matthew asked the one cop.

"No," the cop said.

"Well, there's a first time for nearly everythin'."

He slept in the waiting room on a bank of chairs and when they put Maryanna in a room it was pale morning. A young nurse woke him and he walked the hallways until he found the room and then he slept the morning in fits, propped up in a chair near her bed. He left but once to eat and on the way back to the hospital there were inch-wide snowflakes melting on the windshield of his car. That night the snows came and they covered all.

*

HER TRUCK WAS FULL WITH CARDBOARD boxes and milk crates and the last of the furniture worth keeping. Matthew had already run two truckloads into town and the new landlord helped him get the heaviest pieces into the first floor walk-up. It did not seem like a lot even with just the few of them working. They'd an early spring thaw and the sidewalks and streets in town were all sand and roadgrit. At the cabin grounds there were snows yet in the ditches and trailheads. The passway was mush and had to be travelled slowly.

Maryanna sat on the porch steps and smoked awhile, still very thin, the top of her left ear lost. She fiddled with it often. In the clearing before her sat boxes and boxes of ill-packed junk. Old trophies and some framed black and whites and a stringless guitar stuffed into its own box, pushing the cardboard oblong. Her bed sat out there in the dirt, as did most of her bedroom furniture. Black garbage bags piled high atop the boxspring and full with men's clothes.

Matthew stood one foot to the porch steps and waited.

"I did not think I would live in that town again," Maryanna said.

"Yeah, well."

She stubbed out and started to rise, one hand firm to the stairwell rail. Matthew took her by the forearm and pulled her up the rest of the way. Let go. She brushed off the ass of her pants and walked down amongst the things in the yard. She had a hitch in her step now and always would. She still had the big toe of her right foot but the rest were taken in surgery. Maryanna wore thin boat shoes with stuffing in the one.

"Anythin' left in there?" Matthew said.

"Nope, but take a lap if you want, son."

"What about this shit?"

"The Sally Ann is gonna send a truck this afternoon. We don't gotta wait for them."

Matthew nodded.

"You want to keep anything of his?" she said. "It's okay if you do."

"Hell no," he said.

Matthew went through the house quick. It looked very, very small by the empty rooms and it had been scrubbed to the bone. Hard sun through the naked windows. He didn't linger and when he banged out through the door he didn't lock the place. Maryanna got him as he passed and took his arm and they went across the lot to the truck. Matthew helped his mother up behind the wheel and then he went around to the passenger side. She blew clean and started the engine. Turned back but once before they broke the treeline. Matthew studied her as she drove. She swore the foot did not cause her much grief.

MONTANA BORDER

H E DROVE INTO LAFAYETTE AT DUSK, the air thick with swamp bugs outside the windows of his truck. The fights were already on. They'd put the cage up in an old VFW hall and the beer stalls around the edges of the place were not licensed and neither were the fights. Daniel parked the truck and went toward a service door with a duffle bag of his gear. Bikers were running the door with one gigantic black man in a shirt and tie. That man took some time to find Daniel's full name on the ledger and it had been spelled as wrong as you could spell it. They let him in and he had but half an hour to warm up and take his walk.

THE MAN HE FOUGHT HAD A BEARD and a bald head with old scars run through his scalp. He might have been two hundred and thirty pounds. Daniel weighed just over two hundred by the time he put his mouthguard in and climbed up into the cage. Both fighters wore four-ounce gloves and cups over their junk. They were announced by megaphone to a crowd of howling drunks. The ring announcer fucked up Daniel's last name again and said he was from Columbia, Canada. Daniel barely heard it for the blood that rushed to his ears.

At the bell Daniel tried to take the centre of the cage but the other fighter hustled in low and flat-footed. He loaded up and threw wild, looping shots. Held his breath all the while. Daniel backed out on an angle and push-kicked the man with the ball of his lead foot, shoved him clear. The man came back. Daniel stood him up with a jab and tried to follow with his right but the man blocked it and got hold of him and tried to tie him up in the clinch. Nothing but raw strength and grunts and sweat. Daniel jock-eyed for position and got his hands clasped behind the man's head. The bigger man tried to shuck him but he couldn't and Daniel drove a knee into the man's guts, his hips and ass behind it. All the air went out of the other fighter but he didn't drop. He let his hands fall. Daniel dropped a heavy downward elbow across the bigger man's brow. Another to the man's sidejaw. Daniel tried to follow up but the man wasn't there.

He'd gone down like someone hit the off button and now he lay there limbstretched on the mat. Eyes wound back in his head. His forehead had opened up when the elbow first landed and there was red all over the man and all over the matting. Daniel walked the cage perimeter and people were hollering at him and throwing cans of beer at the stage. He quit circling and went to his corner and knelt there and watched the doctor work on the other fighter.

DANIEL TOOK HIS PAY IN AN envelope. Five hundred dollars and a hotel room key. He had his street clothes on and thumped a beer quick and then he left. Out in the parking lot he met a man wearing a ball cap and cowboy shirt and that man paid Daniel his winnings from a bet he'd had the man make for him. Daniel counted the bills.

"I heard them calling it five to one when I got here," he said.

"The line moved."

Daniel eyeballed the man a second and the man didn't seem to care for it much. He had his thumbs hooked in the back of his belt.

"Sure it did," Daniel said.

Neither said another word but they shook hands. Daniel got in his truck with his gear. He did not go to the hotel and he did not stay the night in that state.

HE WOKE IN HIS TRUCK AND he'd sweat through his clothes. The sun had pulled up and hung full in the window frame. He'd left the glass down in the night and a grasshopper had settled on his shin and sat there fiddling. Daniel lifted his leg and scooted his ass toward the truck door and laid the crook of his knee joint over the framing. He kicked the bug loose. Sting of hot metal on the skin of his calf. He got his leg back inside and sat up. There were miles and miles of cornfield outside the driver door and a near-empty stretch of highway opposite. He stripped to just his gitch and leaned back against the seat. Counted bruises on his arms and on his chest and at his stomach. Knots in his right elbow like healed-over gravel.

Daniel got out of the truck and stood there pissing in the ditch. A car of farm girls went by and one of them hollered so hard that his piss cut out and he had to wait a second to start it going again. He stepped light in the roughgrass to the bed of the truck and dug through his duffle for clean clothes. When he found them he stood there holding them and scoped the sun under the flat of his hand. He put some deodorant on and took the clothes into the truck and dropped them on the passenger seat and pulled out from the shoulder. He drove townward in his skivvies with a bare, bone-sore foot working at the pedals.

HE LAY ON A WOODEN BENCH in the warm-up room. Cinder-block walls painted over blue. As he dozed there were two other fighters hitting pads, one a heavyweight. Daniel half heard the leather taking mitts and shins. After a long while an official came in by the door and the heavyweight went out. Not fifteen minutes later the man came back with his eye shut and bleeding, his nose squashed. The smaller fighter who'd been at the pads slowed up and his cornerman whacked him upside the head. Soon they left out to take the walk as well.

Daniel sat up and took off his hoodie and his socks. The heavyweight watched him sidelong with the one good eye. A doc had come in to examine the man.

"It's like the fuckin' state wrestling team out there," said the heavyweight. "Them against all the fighters come in from elsewhere."

"That's how it always is," Daniel said.

"Well, fuck," the heavyweight said.

HE SPENT THE FIRST ROUND ON his back, the wrestler atop him with his head drove into Daniel's left ear. The wrestler stuck him with elbows and short punches to the body. Partway through the round Daniel started talking at him. The wrestler tried to posture up and thump him but Daniel had control of his wrists and the man couldn't land clean. At the bell the ref touched them both by the shoulder and the wrestler got up slow.

Early in the second round Daniel found his range and pumped a stiff jab in the wrestler's mug over and over, tattooed the man's forehead with it and snapped his head back. When the wrestler tried to shoot in for a takedown Daniel sprawled back and stuffed it, pushed the wrestler down by the back of his head. The wrestler had Daniel's foot but Daniel shucked loose and circled out, drilled him with a straight right and then a left hook as the man got up. Blood from the wrestler's lip and nose. Tired-dog look in his eyes. When next he shot in, Daniel had his timing and stepped in to meet him and put a knee to his mouth. It felt like he'd hit a sack full of light bulbs. The wrestler fell flat and lay there. Daniel loped low and belted him upside the ear with another left hand. The ref pushed him clear and covered the downed man, waved the fight off. Quiet in the arena save for a few fans clapping and whistling in the back seats.

NEAR MIDNIGHT DANIEL SAT on a hay bale beside the wrestler. Farm party lit by truck headlamps with one rig blasting Johnny Cash. Some people came by to talk at them or shake their hands. Many wouldn't. The wrestler had lost two front teeth in the fight but they were fakes. He had them in his breast-pocket of his shirt. They were passing a bottle of bourbon back and forth. Someone had lit a massive bonfire from old wooden pallets and fruit crates in the clearing before an ancient barn. Nobody could get within twenty feet of it and by the fringes of the clearing the cornstalk leaves were curling.

"Ain't that really fuckin' dangerous?" Daniel asked the wrestler.

"Oh, yeah," the wrestler said.

DANIEL WOKE UP IN THE REAR BEDROOM of a trailer with a girl's forearm across his stomach. He had no clothes on and she wore his T-shirt and not a stitch other. His dick was hard and he felt funny with it just out there in the open, the one bedsheet wound up in the girl's legs. He stared up at the ceiling and tried to get his shit together. The girl beside him had auburn hair and a tiny lip ring, pretty as could be with her little make-up and freckles by her cheeks and along the line of her collarbone. He got clear of the arm slow and moved a pillow under it. No matter. She slept like the dead and her nose whistled.

THE COP'S KNUCKLES GOT HIM UP again, over and over on the truck window. When Daniel sat up the cop took a good step back and watched him. Daniel looked around his resting spot at the highwayside and car after car spat past and carried on to wherever. He blinked hard and wound the window down. The cop came back. After a second he leaned in with his forearms on the metal sill.

"Long night?" the cop said.

"Yes sir," Daniel said.

"You know you can't just pull over and squat on the side of a busy goddamn road like this, right?"

"I do now."

"Uh huh," the cop said. "You get into some trouble, son?"

"No sir."

"You been in a scrap?"

"It was a legal one."

"At the arena?"

"At the arena," Daniel said.

The cop nodded and tilted his hat back a little bit. He started toward his cruiser.

"Just take it on down the road," the cop said. "The state line's that way."

Daniel watched him go and then he turned the key and tried to fire the engine. It picked up on the third try. He took off.

HIS LAST FIGHT OF THAT YEAR WAS ON a ranch in northernmost Montana, the cage put together atop two flatbed trailers. Portable bleachers set up around the clearing. Three hundred people saw Daniel get his brow split open by an accidental head-butt and they saw him bleed all over the matting and all over the other fighter. He wrestled the other man to the ground and in the scramble got behind him with his stomach to the man's back, hooked both heels under his quads. The man tried to turn out but couldn't and they were both facing the sky. With red pooling in his left eye Daniel slid his arm under the man's throat and all the sweat and the blood made it hard for the man to grab his gloves and fight off the choke. When he cinched it in the man didn't have time to tap and there he went to sleep.

They had the cut dressed and taped by a cattle veterinarian. The vet offered to stitch the wound but Daniel wouldn't let him. Instead Daniel took his truck and his gear off the ranch and drove the twenty miles to the Alberta border. Where he crossed, the guard in the booth was asleep but the truck motor got him to stir. Daniel showed his passport. The guard asked about the cut and Daniel told him the truth.

"They didn't see to it there?" the guard said.

"If they messed it up it'd never be right again. I figured I'd better come back."

The guard studied him long. Daniel waited with the windows down. Plain winds whistled by and they carried the scent of dewgrass. Somewhere beyond the pass there were coyotes crying.

AT TRIAGE HE GAVE HIS HEALTH CARD and other particulars to a rather pretty middle-aged woman who looked to have not slept in days. If there were a way to be less interested than she was, he couldn't figure out what it might look like. He sat in a row of chairs near to a busted pop machine. Only one other person sat in that room and he was likewise alone and looked Daniel over but once. A minute later that man was sleeping, chin to chest. He had his arm slung to his shoulder with a tied-off pair of corduroys. Daniel did not see any blood.

There was just the one doctor in the place and he came by Daniel's bed to examine the cut. After that he fetched a nurse and she came in through the curtain with a basin full of gauze pads and a plastic bottle of antiseptic. Red, red hair that hung about her shoulders. She sat at the edge of the bed beside him and went to work on the gash. A few seconds passed with her that close and he realized he'd been holding his breath. He'd no way to explain it to himself except that he'd never had feelings just like those before or at least not all in a row. She did not seem to mind him at all.

"Where'd you do it?" she said.

"Pardon?"

She pointed at his brow.

"At work," he said.

"I'm told it was someone head-butted you."

"That's where I work," he said.

The girl took the gauze pad off and studied the cut, his face, the whole of the man. She pushed in the tip of his nose with her index finger.

"How many times you break this?"

Daniel shifted on the bed.

"Just twice. I got it fixed the first time, but it kind of kept getting bashed so the second time I let it stay broke."

The nurse got up and threw the soiled pads away. She'd lain the anesthesia needle and the stitching needle on the counter and she took up the first. Flicked the cylinder and pushed a dribble of anesthetic through the bevel. Daniel saw her back through the scrubs, the knobs of her ankles. She told him to lie down on the bed. When she came over he saw the needle and sat back up.

"Wait," he said.

"You gotta be fucking kidding me," she said.

He started trying to talk her out of it but she put her one hand to his chest and pushed him back down. She sat in the bed beside him and leaned low and stuck him.

TWO DAYS LATER HE WAS BACK at triage. The red-haired nurse passed by while he was filling in his forms. She came over and sat in the chair beside him.

"Hey Sarah," he said.

The nurse read his forms and his chickenscratch. His address in a city some two hours' drive from there. She looked him over.

"My foot hurts," he said.

She tried not to smile but she did.

HE KEPT COMING BACK WITH HIS complaints and traumas until Sarah let him wait out her shift and follow her to eat. They went to a diner with Formica everything and broken neons outside that had long gone dark. They ordered eggs and bacon and sausages each and she ordered a beer. He asked for a Diet Coke.

"I'm not drinking beer alone," she said.

Daniel switched to beer.

"Not much of a drinker," he said. "Plus I got to drive."

"Well, we'll see," she said.

"See what?"

"How far you got to drive."

They ate plenty and Daniel wolfed it down. The nurse didn't lag too far behind and Daniel could barely believe it. He had her by about eight inches and eighty pounds. She'd tied her hair back and a draft tickled at it from the poorly sealed windows. Outside on the plain there were no lights and no lights and then a blinking radio tower firing once every three seconds or so. There were only two other people in the place and they were cops. The one drank a coffee and the other had his head buried in his arms at the tabletop, patrolman's hat listed to his shoulder and propped up straight to his temple. He seemed to be asleep.

They drank a few more beers and talked. She was from the Maritimes and her folks were still out there. Daniel told her where he was from and that he had a half-brother somewhere. Didn't know him. That was all. She ordered another round of beers and asked for the bill.

"You make any money at what you do?" she said.

"I did lately."

She slid him the bill and he put his huge, ruined palm over the paper. He went for his wallet.

"Hang on," she said.

A few minutes later the cops mustered and the one put his hat on right and stretched. They walked out without paying a dime and got in their cruiser and took off down the roadway. Sarah touched the back of Daniel's hand over the bill and got up. She went to the waitress and handed her some money. The waitress pushed through a swinging door to the kitchen and came back a minute later with a crate of beer and set it on the counter. Daniel stood and brought the check over. He paid it and then he took up the crate.

HE HAD A LICENSED FIGHT IN SURREY against the only man who'd ever beat him. Daniel's legal record was twelve and one but the other fights were so many that he had trouble remembering them all. The where of them. How they ended or how bad. The cage had been set up in a hockey arena and there were fighters on the card being groomed for the big show. Daniel and his old buddy were the top fight on the undercard.

In the fight he got hit so hard that his molars sang. He managed to tie the other fighter up and tried to shove him into the cage fencing. The man was older than him and the stronger man by far. Daniel lost the first round but wore little of it on his face. He was losing the second round right to the last minute and there he put a one-two through the other man's guard and sat him down. People stood at ringside. The other fighter scrambled up and Daniel got him to brawl in the middle of the cage. They were each blasting the other until the man's knee hit the mat and he got up again and started to back up. Daniel threw off-time hooks that split the man around the eyes and he beat him limp where the fence met the mat. The ref was slow to get there and Daniel did not quit until he did.

He took the hotel room that night and filled the bathtub with water and bucket after bucket from the ice machine. When he got in with his contusions and knotted shins and shrunk dick he could not catch his breath enough to howl.

THROUGH FOOTHILL LANES HE drove with monstrous trees either side of the road. The engine struggled some on the grade as Daniel went deeper and deeper in-country and he talked to it until they hit the flats near his hometown. There were stoplights there from the seventies and rusted filling station signs that spun atop their pillars or didn't spin anymore. A lot of storefronts were empty and some were boarded over with plywood. One had a picnic table through it and actually balanced mid-window in the glass somehow. Daniel passed a lot of kids he didn't recognize and liked that very much. He even waved to some. One set of girls gave him the finger.

The little house sat plumb in wild thatch as tall as the truck. The gravel driveway was all but gone and there were holes under the lip of the roof where critters made their beds. Somebody had tagged the entire side of the house with a fucked up pentagram, drawn as if by a child on a lot of glue. Daniel took up a rock from the end of the clay trail where he'd parked and pitched it through the empty front door-frame. Hollow banging where the stone travelled. A squirrel blew out from under the eavestrough and went sideways into the trees. Daniel waited a minute and then he trod the brush and went inside.

The living room had holes in the floorboards and there were little bodies huddled in there, eyes aglow and one animal hissed at him. He told it to shut up. Not a scrap of furniture or carpeting left in the place. All the metals had been pulled and there were striplines in the wall where the wiring got torn out. The plumbing was likewise gone by the looks of it, all but a tub of infinite weight planted there in the bathroom, no walls left to close it in. When he got to his parents room there was a door still hung and he went cold. He stared at it awhile and then he toed it with his boot and it drifted open on its hinges. The ceilings and floor were still there and hadn't rotted through. The window in that room had no coverings nor glass and light shone weird to the hardwood. A bedframe alone and flush to the wall. Daniel leaned in for the door and pulled it shut.

He got to the other bedroom and it just wasn't there. The joists were exposed with rusted nails stuck in them and crooked toward the yard. Down three feet from the hole lay bits of wood and stuffing and some plastics that he couldn't identify. Daniel scoped the wildgrass clearing and the woods beyond and the treeline was nearer than he thought it would be. He turned and went back through the place and then he left.

SARAH HAD BEEN IN AND OUT OF BED in the mornings while he lay there knackered. She'd come back to him and put her head by his chest and her breath came too fast where it tickled his skin.

"Are you okay?" he'd ask.

"I'm just out of whack from working nights. It'll pass," she'd say.

If he pressed her about it she climbed him or she kicked him out. Daniel had a week there and then he had to go back north to train for a fight he'd taken on too soon but needed bad. When he left her on her driveway that last day she held on to him too long and he started to hug her all over again. He backed out slow and she was barefoot on the gravel with her eyes hard on him. Daniel waited in the road until she waved and when he drove off he went very slow and his guts were in knots that didn't loose for hours.

HE DROVE ACROSS THE MONTANA BORDER with the sun risen pale behind a grey sky. There were rains that had travelled ahead of him and left the asphalt black and slick. Not far into the state he caught a pool of water and hydroplaned, felt the truck go weightless and drift sideways. When the tires touched dry road the truck bucked hard and fishtailed the other way. Daniel swore shit he'd never heard of and then had the truck straight in the lane again. Nobody else was out there with him and there were no towns nor filling stations for miles ahead or miles behind. He slowed to the speed limit and turned the radio loud. He knew the song and even sang it in a piss-poor tenor, let the words of it rattle in his brain and take up room.

His motel room was the corner unit of a one-level shithole just outside the town of Boulder. Daniel had driven long and checked in but didn't unpack anything. He slept shallow and woke early. They did the weigh-ins at noon and they were meaningless. In bouts where the fighters were coming in heavy they were switched to catch-weight fights before anyone ever got on a scale. Two fighters refused and they were cut out of the card and their opponents paired up instead.

Near midnight Daniel made his walk in suffocating humidity. He had no shirt on and no socks either and sweat pooled in his shoes. They were outdoors except for a kind of pavilion that country bands usually played under. Mosquitoes ate his shoulders and a cloud of gnats turned itself inside out near to where the fighters stood to have their cups and mouthguards checked. Daniel poured water over his head and his chest and when he got to the staging area they wiped him dry again with towels.

Early in the first round Daniel caught the other fighter in an armbar, the man chest-down to the mat with his shoulder trapped. Daniel had the arm fully extended and felt the elbow joint pop between his cup and the canvas. The man didn't tap but he couldn't fight anymore and they called it. There were people in the crowd who knew Daniel's name and when he went back up the makeshift corridor he signed a drunk guy's ball cap and the shirt of a twenty-something girl with both her arms sleeved in tattoos. She said something in Daniel's ear but he didn't hear it.

In the side lot to the place, he met his bookie. The man was tall and had a nasty kind of skinniness about him. He gave Daniel his winnings and they were plenty. Not a dollar had been skimmed.

"That fella's brothers are lookin' for you," the bookie said. "I'd clear outta town."

Daniel nodded and the man put out his hand. Knobbled joints there and the digits far too long. Daniel shook it quick and left the lot. Twenty feet from his truck he turned and there were three bikers trailing him in their leather cuts.

HE DROVE BACK INTO LETHBRIDGE NOT twelve hours later and he'd done it with only his left hand. He couldn't make a fist with the other. Part of an incisor buried in the meat between his first two knuckles. There were scratch marks by his eyes and left cheek as if he'd gone through a hedgerow blind. Otherwise Daniel was whole and bang awake when he pulled into Sarah's drive. He didn't see her car and he didn't know what shift she might be on. He got out and went up the steps.

The apartment had been emptied. Everything but a milk crate filled with trinkets, pop bottles from the fifties, a license plate. Daniel stood in the entryway and had to lean against the framing for a second. He went through the place room by room and then came back into the living room and stared at the milk crate. After a minute he picked it up and flung the contents toward the corner. A bottle broke. He flipped it and set it on the floor. There he sat on the upturned crate and studied the pale walls. He went into his pockets for his phone. He didn't have it.

AT THE HOSPITAL THE TRIAGE NURSE wouldn't tell him anything at first.

"You want me to admit you?"

"No," he said. "I just need to know where she's got to."

The nurse just looked at him.

"She's pregnant," he said.

"I know."

The nurse looked around the place. There was not another soul in earshot.

"She'll likely have gone to her folks," she said. "That's all I can say."

"Yeah?"

"Wouldn't you?"

"No," he said. "I don't know."

Daniel waited at the counter and leaned on it with his forearms. He didn't have a plan about what to do next but the nurse wouldn't shoo him. He had blood dribbling out of his one nostril and she handed him a tissue.

"Well, I guess can someone at least dig this tooth out of me?" he said, and stuck his right fist under the Plexiglas for the nurse to see. She covered her mouth and just stared at the hand. She told him to have a seat.

THERE WERE CHOPPERS RUNNING THE main street by early evening and they were too many to be from the local chapters. They were doing parallels in the roads and circling each neighbourhood. Two or three bikes parked in front of every tavern and motel office. Daniel got back to Sarah's apartment at dusk and drove the truck through the gap between that building and the one beside it, the side mirrors folded back and just an inch or two clear on either side of the vehicle. He wheeled into the courtyard behind and parked in the middle of it where he could not find a sightline from any of the outlying streets.

He lay in the corner of the room on a sleeping bag and used his dirtied clothes for a pillow. The drapes were gone and silver moonlight showed the floor but none of him. He dared not sleep but he was bone-tired and weak with it and soon his head bobbed and went cheek-down to the makeshift bedding. Next he woke and heard scratching at the front door, metal working the keyhole. Daniel slid out from the bed and crawled the room face-down until he passed the door. He stood up slow and waited there.

When she stepped into the room she had a shotgun held low at her hips. Daniel went for her and she turned and froze him up with the barrel and he staggered back in a duckwalk and fell. Where he came to rest his shoulders and his head were partway through the drywall under the kitchen divider. Sarah turned the gun barrel away and stood for a moment with her eyes closed, one hand to her heart.

"Sweet fucking Jesus," she said.

THEY SPENT THAT NIGHT ON THE FLOOR, close together with the scattergun full of double-aught buck and their baby in Sarah's belly. In the small hours they heard an engine growling low and mean. Daniel reached for the gun but Sarah took it up instead. Truly he did not know what to do with it anyway. The world went quiet except for their breathing and the chopper didn't come back for another pass.

"How long do we wait here?" Sarah said.

"'Til dawn I think, and we take your car."

Sarah nodded. She asked him to lie back and he did and she put her head to his chest, the shotgun close by on the floor tiles. She lifted his bandaged right hand and then cupped it over in the both of hers.

"If it turned out to be a boy, would you teach him to fight?" she said.

"I don't know," he said. "Probably I wouldn't like to."

"Maybe it is a boy."

"I damn well hope not."

Outside the moon had gone and they lay in almost pure dark and kept tugging at each other every now and then. Neither would let the other sleep. They had hours to wait yet.

TO HAVE TO WAIT

THEY CAME OUT OF THE HOUSE with the risen sun beating down on the weather-worn porch. The summer had come early this year. The heat burnt the grass brown and took the nearby river down a foot by June, the high watermark lying naked on the granite banks. Paul went down the porch steps with a plastic cooler that had their lunch inside. He stopped on the gravel driveway and had to squint to see. There were waves of heat trembling atop the hot black mastic of the bordering concession road, the air fat with humidity and hard to draw in. It felt as if his nose and throat and very insides ran hotter with every breath he took. He shook his head and stood there, tall and thin, his dark hair flattened down by the dampness of his scalp.

"Shut that door behind you," he called back without turning around. "And make sure it shuts. That mangy farm dog got in there one night and Mum lost her damn mind."

Matthew came out with his shirt half on and he was still wet from the shower. When he pulled the T-shirt down it darkened in patches, sitting ridged and crooked across his heavy chest. He left it like that and pulled the door shut as he came out. He took a step and then stopped and went back. He gave the door a shove. It came open so he leaned back inside and grabbed the knob and pulled as hard as he could. This time he heard the metal latch click. The door stayed put when he shoved it again.

"That door's a piece of shit," he said, coming down the steps in ragged old skateboard shoes. When he got down to the gravel he trod heavy on the rocks and they shot clear as he walked past Paul to the passenger side of the car. Matthew tried to open the door and it wouldn't give. He stared down at the handle and muttered something, his hand still trying it. His fingers kept going even when he knew the door was locked and finally he stopped and put both arms on top of the roof. Inside of a second he yanked them clear and cursed a string of nonsense at the car and the heat and the world altogether.

"It's hot as absolute hell out here," Matthew said. "This car is going to be a billion fucking degrees inside."

Paul nodded and spat on the ground. The phlegm was thin and parts of it started to vanish right away on the stone. He exhaled hard and went over to the car and stood facing his brother, both of them the same height, Matthew much larger in build. They had the same eyes though, the same hairline. They had the same shape of mouth and sometimes made the same expressions on very different faces, Paul's thinner face with its squared jaw and Matthew's rounded face with a rounded jaw and that thick, wide-set neck below it. They looked at each other awhile. Paul's eyes were clear, though they skittered around. Matthew's eyes, bloodshot from the drink, were still as the burnt and breezeless world around them.

"Was Mum outraged last night?" Matthew said.

"She didn't say one way or the other," Paul said, "but I guess you probably could have come back here first to drop your shit off. Instead of straight from the airport to the bottle."

"I know. I should've."

"I talked her down though, before she took off for work. Told her you'd be back to the house this morning to go with me an' that you'd see her tonight. I also told her your future wife was likely at the party. That you might shack up with some townie and quit your fuckin' philandering."

Matthew stood there with his mouth part open. He blinked hard and his eyelids were out of sync. Paul started laughing at him.

"You're still plastered, you idiot."

Little laughs came out of Matthew's maw for a few seconds, and then he inhaled hard and stood up straight.

"You should've come out last night."

"I'd say I'm sort of way past partied out. It's not so bad when you just come back home for a little while and cause some shit. But when you live here you'd rather punch yourself in the dick than go out with those idiots."

"You just didn't go 'cause you couldn't have driven today. You'd be in bed 'til five with your hangover."

"I have to drive 'cause your license is suspended."

"It's suspended 'cause I was driving your unin-sured fuckin' car when you were too hung over."

Paul looked at Matthew for a second and then turned away. He nodded. When he turned back he had a crooked little smile on his face.

"Yeah, I know," he said. "We'll sort that out too."

Paul put the key in the lock and turned it, then opened the door. The heat inside swarmed him. He made a funny sound and hit the button to unlock all the doors. Matthew still couldn't get in.

"Stop fuckin' pulling on it," Paul said.

This time when Paul hit the button Matthew's door unlocked and he opened it. He leaned back from the car when he felt the air and then he took a deep breath. He looked over at Paul and they shook their heads and got in. Paul put the key in the igni-tion and turned it, and they wound down their win-dows before shutting the doors.

"I don't care about losin' the license," Matthew said. "I don't even have a car."

Paul looked over at him and nodded. Then he turned the radio on.

"Yeah, but you might have one someday," Paul said.

"Fuck it. I ride the bus. I'm gonna get a bike maybe."

Paul smiled. "Man, you'll die riding a bike in that city."

"I don't die doing anything," Matthew said. "And it sure as fuck wouldn't be in that city." He let out a short, loud laugh.

Paul fished a bottle of water out of a cooler in the back seat and drank deep. Matthew waited for him to pass it over, and all the while he stared through the front windshield at the house they'd grown up in. The narrow two-storey farmhouse stood at the head of the driveway, simple and ancient. If it had not been handed down to their family with the outlying fields and firs they would have had little at all. Not ten years ago those boys had set down to eat a mess of bacon and egg and fried steak in the damp, stone-walled kitchen, their parents gone for the night. The greasy plates had just hit the suds in the sink when a black sedan rolled into the driveway carrying five men, all of them bent on laying Matthew out and stomping him bloody into the gravel. Paul racked rocksalt shells into an old double-barrel scattergun and went out to meet them. By the time he had come back inside Matthew had soaked a rag through with spirit, had jammed it into the bottleneck, and was trying to spark it with a barbeque lighter. Paul wrestled the bottle from his brother and cursed him out until Matthew sat down at the kitchen table and put his head in his hands. He was sixteen years old. Paul was just two years older. Later that night they drank the bottle dry, sitting together in the dark waiting for the men to locate their guts and come back. They never did.

"You miss that house?" Paul said.

"I don't know. It's hard to believe I lived in it."

"What's it like out there where you live?"

"Like Mars."

"You gonna ever come back east?"

"I think so."

"When?"

"As soon as I made enough money to live off the bullshit wages back here. Or as soon as they start throwin' money at people with grade twelve who can dig the hell out of a pipeline ditch."

Paul smiled. Matthew turned to face him.

"You could live with me when I move back," he said. "Get a cheap place somewhere in a town that ain't this one."

"I like it here."

"Nobody likes it here. Not anybody smart as you."

Paul shrugged.

"In a world that wasn't so fuckin' silly," Matthew said, "I'd be able to stomach being here while you took another run at that college. Even with no money and old enemies gettin' fat just down the road."

Paul nodded but he didn't say anything. Matthew shifted in his seat. He spat out of the window and hung his head.

"Truth be told, man, this place makes my fuckin' skin crawl. I don't feel right until I get ten miles past the township line."

Paul backhanded sweat from his brow, wiped his hand on the seat cover.

"This place wasn't ever kind to you," he said.

Pointing west, Matthew said, "Out there I do okay. I ain't shit in this town."

"You are right now. Trust me."

Matthew shook his head.

"Of all the days to be here," Paul said, "This is the one."

He fiddled with some of the levers and knobs on the console. Then he gave the dashboard a whack with his right hand and the air conditioning came on.

"Yes," Matthew said.

"You want to get out and wait until it cools down?" Paul said.

Matthew looked at him and then looked past him out of the driver-side window at the fields of high-grass, the hazy outline of pine trees rising from the slope of the mountains to the north.

"No," he said. "Let's get going. He'll be waiting for us to get there. I don't want him to have to wait."

Paul nodded and put his seatbelt on. Matthew sat back in his seat and shifted some more. He pulled at his shirt and seemed to make it more crooked by trying to fix it. Paul studied his brother for a few seconds, then put the car into gear.

"Okay," he said.

THEY DROVE ALONG THE SINGLE-LANE county roads to avoid the traffic, the tourists, and travellers. They passed farms with empty fields and others with crops of corn and soy, new metal silos lit up by the sunlight and old wooden barns gone to rot. They saw very little cattle. There were horses grazing close to the road on one property, one head sticking out through the wire of the perimeter fence, the ears flicking. Soon the car followed the rear boundary of another field. This time the fencing was reinforced by wooden slats, and there were some high sheetmetal walls with barbed wire running along the top. Way off in the distance the field went up a hillside and there were strange shapes moving out there, creatures that were too tall or ran on two long legs, and some with horns that no animal from that part of the world should have. Matthew mouthed a profanity and squinted as he tried to figure out what he was watching out of his window. Suddenly he started nodding and turned to his brother. Paul had been older when they were there last and he'd known the place right away. He started to laugh. Matthew frowned at him and turned back. They observed a battered wooden sign with something like a tiger's head painted on it. "Elmvale Jungle Zoo," it said. Matthew watched the sign go by and shook his head as it went.

"That place is retarded."

"Remember when that tiger got out and went into the town and the cops came in and shot it before anyone could get to it with the tranquilizer gun?"

"No," Matthew said.

"Man, I do."

Matthew wouldn't stop shaking his head. When they had long since cut through the township he still had a troubled look on his face. Paul knew his brother wasn't fretting that hard about the ramshackle zoo. He waited and soon enough Matthew spoke up.

"How has she been without him there?" he said.

Paul held the wheel in one hand and ran the other through his hair. He wiped a palmful of sweat on his shirtsleeve.

"You know, you take for granted the kind of feelings they got for each other, forget they been through shit that would kill most folks," Paul said. "Then you see one of them without the other.... Shit."

"Yeah."

Paul bit at his nails, then put his free hand back on the wheel.

"She goes to work and she fusses around the house and gets on with it, but there's nothing behind it.

All those old routines don't mean shit anymore. They just pass the time."

"What about when he was home?"

"Before, when he was there between the treatments, he wasn't really himself. They put you under and hit you with that juice and it saps the life right outta you. He came home worn out. Couldn't remember a lot of things. It was weird. So this last time he asked just to stay in there until it was done."

Matthew leaned back in his seat and set his arm on the windowledge. His skin stuck to the plastic. Then he too wiped his brow with his T-shirt. He coughed and had to roll down the window to spit. A torrent of warm air came in at them. Matthew shut his eyes and took a deep breath.

"You might as well leave that open," Paul said. "This air conditioner hasn't done shit for us in its life."

Paul also put his window down and they drove for a long time with nothing but the sound of the rushing wind and the low wail of the radio through the car speakers. Paul thought Matthew had gone to sleep until his brother sat up straighter in his seat and wound his window halfway up and sat there scratching his head. Paul rolled his window partway up as well.

"How do those things work? Those treatments?" Matthew said.

"They send a current through your brain to make you seizure."

"Does it hurt him?"

"You're out when they do it. They say you don't feel it. But the anesthetic does a number on you. And like I said, you forget shit for a while and you wake up without that fucking awful shit on your mind. That's why epileptics don't get depressed. Their brain hits a point and just says no more and they seizure. Nobody knows for sure how it works."

Matthew took a deep breath and let it out slow. He rubbed at his eyes with the palms of his hands, leaned forward and crossed his arms on the dashboard. Then he rested his chin against them.

"I don't know, man," he said. "Anything with the brain freaks me out. I might rather be depressed than risk it. But you're closer to it than I am. I don't know."

Paul stared out at the open road. The greying tarmac ran straight for miles and miles and shimmered under the blazing sun, and far off on the horizon a fog of humid heat obscured the country ahead. Not one cloud was above them, and he knew they were still far inland and had a long way to go.

"I'd rather have seizures," he said.

Matthew raised his head and stared at Paul for a while but Paul didn't look back.

IN THE EARLY AFTERNOON THEY PULLED into a gas station at the edge of town. There were only two pumps and one of them ran diesel for the tractors and trucks that came through. The station sat in the bottom of a valley where a dozen houses had been built maybe a century ago and half were boarded up or left to slow decay whether people lived in them anymore or not. The two-digit sign that stood high above the lot couldn't keep up with the price of gas, and so now it just read a double zero, the going rate guessed at by those passing through. Paul pulled in from the road and came up to the pump and stopped.

"We runnin' low?" Matthew said.

"We don't know where we are," Paul said. "And yeah, we could use some gas too."

Matthew sat up straight. He rubbed at his face and exhaled hard. Then he opened his door. "You pump, I'll pay," he said.

"Okay."

Matthew went toward the gas station store, his arms stretched out wide, the back of his shirt dark with sweat. Paul waited a second and then got out of the car. He walked around it and stretched his arms as well, blinking under the open sky where the sun sat lonely and ruthless. He took the nozzle out of the pump and flipped the metal switch so that the gas would flow. Then he pulled the nozzle to the rear of the car, the hose tethered to the pump by a line with a rusted metal coil at the end. The gas tank's cap had been lost for years, so he just opened the flap, shoved the nozzle into the hole and squeezed. He thought of something and turned in time to see Matthew open the front door of the station before stepping in.

"Hey," Paul yelled.

Matthew stopped short in the doorway and turned around. He stood there waiting.

"Get us some drinks for the ride back if you want."

Matthew nodded and went inside. Paul looked over at the closing door for a few seconds, turned back to the pump and watched the numbers cranking over, the digits distorted by faulty electronics in the display. He got near enough to the amount he wanted and guessed where to stop, then walked the nozzle back to the pump. He saw what looked like twenty-six dollars and eighty-eight cents worth of gas and let out a little laugh, thinking about Matthew's face when the attendant told him what he owed. Paul went over to the back of the car to shut the gas-tank flap. As he did so he saw three men about his age walking into the lot toward the store. Two of them were wearing ball caps and cargo shorts and the other had short, ragged hair and torn jeans and no shirt on. They all had the rough look of a long night, but they were talking and laughing, so Paul called over to them.

"Hey guys," he said. "How's it going?"

The shirtless man turned as they came by and they slowed up but didn't stop. None of them said anything. They just looked at Paul.

"You guys from around here?" Paul said.

"Yeah," the shirtless one said. "Why's that?"

"I'm just tryin' to figure out how to get somewhere."

"Where you goin'?"

Paul studied the three men for a moment. The two men with caps were taller and they seemed uninterested. One took off his cap to wipe his brow and he had a bad haircut with a bald patch at the centre of his head. The shirtless man was shorter and well-built and he had a cross tattooed across his shoulder, the work poorly done.

"We gotta get to Pineridge. You know the place?" Paul said.

The man smiled. "Yeah, I know it."

"Good."

"What you gotta go there for? Who you got in there?" the man said.

Paul looked into the man's eyes and then he turned and stared out past the gas station lot at the firs that rose up the valley hillside. He cleared his throat and turned back. The man was still waiting for an answer, still grinning. Paul didn't like the man at all.

"So, how do we get there from here?"

"Nobody wants to go out there," the man went on. "People go in there for a reason. They don't come back out. You know that old guy that shot that cop in the head in the bar a couple years back. In front of all those people. He's in there. So's the fucker who did all them kids. All kinds of wackos in there. For real."

"I'm not fuckin' goin' to that part. That's the maximum-security part. He's in the other side. Where you get treated and you get out."

"Who is?" the shirtless man said.

Paul kept staring at the three men, but he didn't have anything to say to them. Now they wouldn't move along. They just stood there smiling and mumbling things to each other, and then Paul heard the creak of the shop door and he saw Matthew coming out with a plastic bag in his hand. Matthew was looking down. He spat on the ground and when he looked up he saw Paul. He hesitated and then went on. Paul turned back to the men and went around the car to the driver-side door and opened it. The shirtless man watched him go, said something to his friends over his tattooed shoulder and kept staring Paul down. Paul still wouldn't say anything more.

"Who you goin' to see in there?" the shirtless man said, "Ain't nobody from around here, that's for sure. They fuckin' set up shop there and bring all these sickos from everywhere and fuck up our town. That place should be burnt to the fuckin' ground with whoever you're goin' to get in it."

Paul shut the door and the shirtless man drew himself up big and held his hands out in waiting. But Paul wasn't looking at him. He was looking at Matthew, who had dropped the bag on the ground and had come up behind the three men.

"Hey," Matthew said.

The shirtless man turned. He was still grinning and didn't see it coming. Matthew dug his feet in and threw a short left hook from the hip and caught the man right on the mouth and the man sat down hard on the sand-strewn asphalt and stared up in utter confusion, blood coming out of his nose in a thin, steady line. Matthew had his right cocked but the shirtless man didn't try to get up and his two friends just stood there. One swore but he didn't move. Matthew looked at each of the two men and back at the downed man. Then he looked over at his brother. Paul had come around the car and stood beside the pump shaking his head.

Matthew raised his eyebrows. "What?" he said.

"Get in the car," Paul said.

Matthew stayed calm as he picked up the plastic bag and sidestepped the three men, the one he'd punched still sitting on the ground with his hand over his nose, blood between his fingers and hate in his eyes. Matthew went over to the car and Paul opened the passenger door and waved him in. As Matthew sat down the door shut behind him. Then he heard the sound of gravel shifting as the man he had hit scrambled up to holler something at them. Matthew turned to Paul, but Paul was already making his way over to the men with his long deliberate strides. Matthew got out of the car but he wasn't quick enough. Paul had already hit the shirtless man three times before Matthew got to him. The man had only been on his feet long enough to say a few words. Now he was lying on the ground again with his hands pawing at the air. If the other men had thought about doing something they gave it up when Matthew came back. He grabbed Paul around the chest with both arms and pulled him away. Once Paul had been dragged clear he shucked loose and started for the car without looking back and without even looking at Matthew. His face was flushed and his teeth tight together and his knuckles were slathered with blood from the man's ruined nose and mouth. The brothers walked to the car together and Matthew had his right arm over Paul's shoulder. His heavy hand lay flat against Paul's chest and Matthew held him close, patting his palm hard against a fast-beating heart.

THE CAR CRESTED THE NORTH RIDGE of the valley by the late afternoon and started down the other side. For a few minutes Paul and Matthew were high above the town, staring out together at the shoreline with its maze of docks and piers and boats coming into their slips and others drifting out into the bay. The water shone green in the sunlight. There were no waves because there was no wind, but the surface shimmered and shifted just so slightly. Far off in the bay were tiny islands of shieldrock and some were topped with dwarf white pines and bowed willow trees. The horizon line lay out in the distant waters and if there was land beyond you couldn't tell it by sight.

"That's a nice place, isn't it," Matthew said.

"It would be."

They could have driven straight through the town but Paul took them around it, coasting down on a zigzag route through the streets until the car came out onto a long, level road that took them past parks and marshes and a massive retrofitted power station before leading right to the bay side of the town. Here they merged into sparse traffic on a four-lane shore-line roadway and drove a little more than a mile east around the outskirts of the north end before leaving the winding coastal road. A large promontory rose up toward the water's edge, blanketed by pines and larger deciduous trees with their foliage burnt and dried above the treeline. Farther up the treecover thinned and there were great, smooth boulders jut-ting out of the hill-face as renegade knobs and joints of the earth's very bones. On the plateau sat an enor-mous modern building made of grey stone and newly forged metal and heavy slabs of glass set together to form a near-seamless westerly roof.

"That's one hell of a fuckin' building," Matthew said. "You really need to make it stick out like that, in case anyone would ever forget it was there in the first place. Jesus."

Paul nodded but he didn't say anything. He had taken to wringing the steering wheel with his hands as he drove and when he saw the sign he was look-ing for he turned left and took the car up the hill-side road. They climbed up to the place under the ever-shifting shadows of the wooded pass and at the top the road flattened out. Paul slowed the car as they came to the front gates. There an old man with a guard's cap and uniform sat in a glassed-in booth and when they pulled up he pushed a button and asked them what they were there for.

"We're going to the northwest wing. To pick somebody up."

"Okay," the man said and relaxed somewhat.

Paul gave their surname and the man said it was alright. He opened the gates and waved them through. Paul nodded and drove on.

"Doesn't take much to get in or out of here," Matthew said.

"That's 'cause people don't care about this part of the place. It's that one there they're worried about."

Paul cocked his thumb toward the passenger side of the car and Matthew looked out of his window. A fork in the road ran toward another set of gates, solid metal doors sealed fast between barricades that stood twenty feet tall with razor wire fixed between spikes at the top. The building that they had seen from the road sat far away behind the barrier. The car followed the gentle curve of the road until they were driving away from the structure. Now they saw another one ahead. It was older and made of limestone and red brick, with dozens of its windows shut except for a few on the lower level beside the main entryway. There were no gates and no guards. They pulled right up to the front steps and Paul put the car in park but he left it running.

"Can you park here?" Matthew said.

Paul just sat there for a moment and then he took a deep breath before opening his door.

"Hey," Matthew said.

Paul turned. "You stay here in the car. If somebody tells you to move then move it."

"I'm coming in there with you. We're gonna get him together."

"It's not like that in there. It won't make it any better. I been in before so I'll go get him. The sooner we get him outta there and on the road the easier it'll be."

"What the fuck are you talkin' about?" Matthew said. "I want to go in there and get him with you."

"Why the hell would you want to do that?"

"What?"

"Listen to me. Stay here. I've seen him in there before. You haven't. He'll remember it that way. Just you being here with him in the car, not in there. It won't make it any better for you to go in."

"What the fuck you mean, 'any better'?"

"It won't make it any better for him."

Paul got out of the car and stood there with the door open. He stared up at the building and then looked west toward the seemingly endless waters. He swore and shut the door and leaned down so he could see in through the open window on the driver's side. Matthew kept looking at him, but he didn't say anything else. Paul nodded. He slapped the edge of the window with his palm and then stood up and walked around the car and started up the stone entryway steps.

"Tell him I'm waiting out in the car," Matthew said.

"Okay," Paul said, but he didn't look back.

When he came back down the steps a few minutes later Matthew was sitting in the back seat. Paul was carrying a small suitcase with their father right behind him at his shoulder. He had gone nearly all grey, though his hair still grew thick. His dark eyes were the same as Paul's, as were his small ears and slender nose and the shape of his chin as well as the narrow shoulders, the wiry arms and legs. If he weren't so much shorter than Paul the future would have seemed utterly foretold. Matthew got out of the car and looked at Paul as he went by to put the suitcase in the trunk.

"Hey Dad."

"Hello son."

Matthew smiled crooked and went over to put his arms around him, the man's chin pushing against his shoulder. His father seemed not to know what to do at first, but soon enough those aged, familiar arms rose and held fast and then he was patting his son's back with his worn-out hands.

THEY DROVE WITH THE SUN SINKING into the Jack pine forest to the west. Paul was still behind the wheel. Matthew sat in the back seat and he could see his father's eyes in the passenger-side mirror and he had never seen their reflection in that mirror before. The three of them had never been in a car at once without their father as the driver. The old man stared out of his window at the fading day and must have seen something there because he sat very still for a long time. When they asked him about the hospital or about his health at all he only gave them a few words back and after he replied he would look away again and seemed to be thinking too long about what he'd said. He appeared eerily calm until he turned to answer another question from Paul and saw the swollen knuckles on his son's right hand.

"What the hell is that?" he said.

Paul shifted in his seat, lifting his hand off the wheel like he might hide it somewhere. There were lies circling about in his head and he glanced up to the rear-view mirror at Matthew for just a second.

"It's nothing."

"Who did you hit? Why did you hit them?"

As he said it he reached out and took Paul's hand in his and examined it close, his own scarred and misshapen fingers going over the damage with great care. Faint red stained into the ridged skin over the knuckle joints. Paul didn't say anything.

"The man needed to be hit," Matthew said from the back seat.

"Matthew," their father said sharply and Matthew went quiet. The man didn't even have to turn around. He looked over at his eldest son and his eyes were wide and full of concern and other things that Paul had never seen there before and couldn't identify. He let go of Paul's hand and shifted back into his seat properly, but he kept his eyes on his son.

"I couldn't help it, Dad," Paul said. "I didn't even think about it."

"Did they hit you first?"

"No."

"What did they do to you?"

Paul ran the injured hand through his hair, then scratched at the back of his neck. After a few seconds he took the wheel again with it.

"They said something about you," he said.

Paul tried to keep his eyes on the road but his father kept studying him. The old man put one of his heavy hands over his mouth and then took it away and bit at his malformed nails. Soon he stopped and looked at his hand and then lay it flat on the windowledge. He stared at it for very long time before he spoke again.

"You can't do that, Paul," he said. "Unless you are in real trouble you can't do it. And never because of me. Someone shits on my name it doesn't make me happy, but I won't have you risk coming to any harm over me, not you or your brother."

In the rear-view mirror Paul saw Matthew rubbing at his chin with his palm. Saw him snort and let out a heavy breath. Paul watched the road and kept quiet. He nodded.

"Paul," his father said. "You promise me that."

He stared at him until Paul looked back.

"Okay."

Paul turned to the road ahead and his father watched after him. Then he reached up and put his hand on his son's neck and squeezed a little. When he let go he did so with some hesitation. Everybody in that car knew that they had heard a promise that would never be kept.

They were all quiet for a long time until Matthew spoke up.

"Dad," he said. "Do you want to stop? You haven't eaten anything."

"If you want to get something then sure, we can stop wherever."

"We're okay, Dad," he said. "It's up to you."

Their father turned and looked at Matthew for a second and then at Paul.

"If you two are okay I'd rather just keep heading for home."

"Sure," Matthew said. "Let's just keep on going. Paul's been driving a long time."

"That's what I figured."

*

THE CAR TURNED ONTO THE COUNTY road in the near dark. There were stars in the sky already and just a shred of the moon and in the dusk there were birds flying in tandem and others perched on the power lines in small groups and a few standing alone. From far down the road they could see the old familiar shape of the wooden farmhouse, the shadows of their clothes rising and drifting out from the metal skeleton of the rotary clothesline in the yard. The breeze that moved them had come in from the north and it played in the trees and when the car crept up to a stop sign they could hear crickets singing in the charred thickets of tall grass and off in the fields the distant sound of a dog barking. They went on through the crossing toward two lights burning, one in the front porch, another in the kitchen.

Matthew slumped against the open window. He hadn't seen his mother in over a year. He stared into the half-light blindly. Inside the house she would be watching their arrival through the window, standing over the sink in her nightgown with a cold bottle of beer on the counter beside her. Their dinner would be on plates in the oven, warming there while she worried about them coming in so late and about the drive that was now over. She would be wondering if they had eaten already while she waited, her appetite lost to nervousness. They would come in and she would fuss about them and say something about them being late and then she would hug their father very hard and Paul and Matthew even harder, as if they had been locked away with him. She might not expect them to eat, but she would lay out their supper and make them sit down at the table, the four of them together. She would take her place last, having waited with the phantoms and the dark corners and the pictures of their long-gone relatives, the part that was missing returned to her and their house made home again.

BANDITS

THE DAY I TURNED EIGHTEEN WE drank a keg of beer between the five of us and let out over the frozen bay in our sleds. Pa on the lead machine with a pump shotgun strapped to the seat, the barrel fitted with a full-choke. His two younger brothers trailing, whooping and swerving wild on the ice over six inches of snow that fell since early evening. My cousin Ronnie coasted wide on his older sled. He had turned twenty-one in the Hillcrest pen. Ronnie was twenty-five now and he was like my brother. Even more so because Pa would thump him silly on the front lawn when he mouthed off or otherwise goaded the big man enough to warrant some violence.

There was a storm coming from the north and you could see the black clouds rolling even against the lesser black of the moonlit sky. Thunder from the heavens and did it ever fucking boom. Next came bolts of white-blue lightning. Smell of electric all over. The snow came down heavy. It looked to me like the end of the world. We passed between two fishing huts and crossed to the other side of the bay, close to the big houses and cottages planted there. Most of them were empty for the season. They were summer homes for people from the city or second houses for the richest in town. Pa throttled down and so did we all. Crept up rumbling aside a fine cedar-wood house with great bay windows, boathouse half as big as our actual house.

Pa turned and untethered the shotgun. Loaded it with double-aught buck and racked a round. He let fly like a marauder on horseback and blasted out two of the front windows. Loaded up again and pulled. Spitfire leapt from the barrel and siding from the west corner of the house blew out in a cloud of jagged timber. Pa gunned it and took off, shotgun held high over his head. He had pocketed his gloves to shoot, and from close by I could see the meatclub that he called his right hand, fingers around the scattergun stock, dark blue ridges of scar tissue and maroon gunk at his skin-split knuckles.

AT FOUR IN THE MORNING WE WERE back at the house, the living room and kitchen in ruin. Pa kept it clean for the most part. It surprised the hell out of people when they came by, expecting a certain measure of filth and disarray. He'd not ever moved any of ma's knick-knacks, pictures, the crosses up on the wall. All were polished and pretty. I didn't have no mother because she died of a brain aneurysm in the middle of the public library, checking out books about eastern rattlesnakes for me for school. I was fourteen. You couldn't set a beer bottle on the coffee table without a coaster or Pa would smash you upside the head with those hamhock mitts of his. You couldn't until the weekend, or a night like this one. And then the place went fairly direct to the boundaries of manmade chaos. By the end of that night there were two of Pa's brothers passed out in our living room. Funhouse versions of my Pa. Uncle Dan on a short couch, his long tree-trunk legs hooked over the end. Uncle Dougie in a chair that extended out with a footrest, spider limbs stretched long, littlest finger of his right hand but a stump. Me and Ronnie were still up, pickled as could be. Pa sat heavy on his armchair with a bottle of rye in his lap.

"I didn' know you'd get lightin'n a snowstore," Ronnie said.

"Well you know it now, eh dipshit? Or you better 'cause you just seen it."

Ronnie made a sour face and his head lolled. Dad leaned out of his seat and got hold of Ronnie by the shirt collar.

"I hear any of this gets back to your mother and I'll beat the living shit out of you."

"I never talk at her 'bout anythin'."

Pa slapped him lightly across the cheek.

"Good," he said. "Lord knows that woman's been through enough. We gotta look after her."

MONDAY MORNING THE COPS came by. Two cruisers rolled up the drive and parked. Constables took their time getting out. I was up eating cold fried chicken at the table and set it down to watch them think about how they were gonna come at the house. One of the cops wasn't Ronnie's age yet and he had his thumb on the clasp of his gun holster. An older cop from the first car turned and saw him. This was a man we knew, tall and thick and beer-bellied, gone grey a long time ago. He stared the young cop down. The young cop didn't seem to know what he was doing.

"You wanna get your fuckin' hand off that pistol," the big cop told him.

So he did.

The big cop pinched the bridge of his nose with his thumb and middle finger, rubbed his eyes. He walked slow to the front steps. Hitch in his step where he'd taken buckshot to the knee as a younger man. The fresh cop followed. I could see the other two start to prowl around either side of the house.

"Don't go far," the big cop said. "I'm tellin' yous."

They came back.

The cop all but filled the doorframe, rapped his knuckles hard against the naked wood of our screen door.

"That you, Charlie?" he said.

"Yep," I said.

"Is your dad around?"

"Who's askin'?"

The cop took off his cap, scratched at his scalp.

"Just get him for me, will ya?"

I went down the hall and opened the door to the garage. Hollered for my Pa over some sixties metal he was blasting, the even-louder whine of an industrial drill. I flicked the lights on and off and the high-pitched drill-screech wound lower. The stereo shut off. Pa came out from behind the stripped-out frame of an old Mercury coupe and walked over, all six-foot three inches and two hundred and forty pounds of him. He had brick dust in his beard and all over his shirtfront.

"One day you do that shit I'm gonna drill something I ain't meant to drill. And you'll be all the sorer for it."

"Fuckin' cops are here."

He stared at me, took up a rag and wrung his hands. He nodded. Came up the shortsteps and into the house. We were eye to eye when he put his huge mitts on either of my shoulders and guided me outta the way. I had his height but by God he was the stronger man by far and I couldn't catch up quick enough.

The cop waited at the end of the porch, leaning heavy against the deck rail. He heard us coming and said something to the other cops. Pa opened the screen door and stood there.

"Francis," he said.

"Rick," the cop said. "Long time."

"Not long enough. What's up?"

They stared at each other. I could see the big cop started to smirk a little.

"Somebody shot up the chief's lakehouse. Banged holes in the place with double-aught buck. Probably lit it up from the ice."

"Did they?"

"You know anybody that might do somethin' like that?"

"I know all kinds of people that might."

LATER ON WE WERE ON THE WAY OVER to Ronnie's place. His mom, my aunt Colette, was fixing us some dinner. We walked the broken-up tarmac of our road, tall firs on either side, pine needles all over the fringe where we trod. It had gone awful fucking cold all of a sudden and I hadn't worn the coat for it. Pa stepped long over the drainage ditch at the roadside and started down a trail through the woods, snow in there flattened by sled runs.

"We shoulda drove," I said. "It's fuckin' freezin' out here."

"It's two minutes away by the path," he said. "Quit your bitchin'."

He had a bottle of whiskey and a bottle of wine in either hand, paper bags crushed and creased over the glass by his bare fingers. The cold didn't seem to bother him ever.

"The cops gonna be a problem?" I asked him. "Them that came by?"

"Nope."

"I went to school with the one of them, the pretty boy, flat-top fucker by the cruiser. He was in his last year when I was in my first. Thinks he's fuckin' God's gift."

"Uh huh."

"I was just gonna tell old Francis at the door to fuck off. Thought that's what you might say, too."

My Pa slowed but he didn't stop. Through breaks in the wood I could see the yellow porch light from my aunt's house. A dog started barking. Clatter of its chain as it tried to get clear of the yard. We turned off the main trail and walked a narrow line toward the place.

"Don't be stupid, son," Pa said.

"How's that?"

"I known that man for near forty years. Since you weren't even a notion. He ain't out there to be a cowboy. He's reliable. Reliable in what he won't do when he's got nothin' on you and reliable in what he will do if he does."

"He just looks like some other cop to me."

"That's because you got shit for brains yet."

"Hey."

"They send cops all like your GI Joe high school buddy and somebody might get shot."

"But not your pal, Francis?"

"He's already been shot. Most men don't get to say that."

He wouldn't talk to me no more after that. We cleared the woods and went through the side yard and that tethered-up mutt came flying at us. Pa stopped it with a look and an outstretched hand, one sausage finger pointing at it from around the whiskey bottle. When we got up on the step he knocked and backhanded the other bottle into my guts. Looked over his shoulder at me.

"Guests bring a fuckin' offerin'," he said. "Make yourself useful."

Near daybreak I woke up with a hangover and a wicked case of dry-mouth. Headache stirring behind my ears. My jeans were still on and I was shivering under my one blanket, the others all piled up on the floor. I went to the bathroom to piss, stepping light on the cold bathroom tiles. Then I walked down to the kitchen for some water and Aspirin. When I passed my Pa's room the door was open, the bed made. The old bastard wasn't any-where to be found.

When I woke up the second time morning was almost spent. I could smell fried-up bacon and coffee at brew. Pa was at the kitchen table with the radio on. He had a platter in front of him with toast crumbs and traces of egg yellow on it. They were playing out the end of a shitty country tune. He turned the volume up.

"There any breakfast for me?" I said.

"There is if you make it. Now quiet down."

The local weatherman told the forecast in his bumpkin rasp. We'd hit minus thirty overnight and it was gonna stay cold through the week. Snow to follow heavy starting early Thursday evening. Pa clapped his hands loud.

"Get yourself a good'un, kid, and eat up. We all got work to do."

WE LEFT OUT FROM THE HOUSE at midnight Thursday. All five of us on our sleds. The two best of them, my Pa's machine and the one his brother Dan rode, they were fitted up with custom tow trailers. Not much more than rude metal boxes with old sled skis welded to the bottom. There were blankets piled up in each and tarpaulin pinned there by rig winch-straps. Pa went first across the ice, led by a good dis-tance and told us stay back a-ways. His rig was the heaviest, and were he to go through, he didn't want us following him down in the deep.

At a point Pa signalled and his youngest brother, Doug, gunned it and took off. He passed the lead sled and kept on until his reflectors were small and then lost to the black. We were all dressed in heavy snow gear, facemasks under our visored helmets. The wind found its way through by nooks and crannies. Cold enough to shrink your sack and make you turn around. Nobody thought on it and if they did they would never have said so. We crossed the ice single file and gapped a good ways between. I couldn't see shit and didn't have a clue where we were at, but Pa did. He knew where the shoreline sat before his headlights showed it. He slowed up and so did we. His sled climbed up a rise and the trailer skittered behind. One by one we left the ice and started down a tree-bound sled trail. They were woods like ours but not all the way, being that we'd driven clear into the next township.

The liquor store sat in a clearing beside the single-lane highway. We came at it from the other side, not a house or traveller met on the way. Pa led us slow to the edge of the site backlot and there we let the sleds idle. The store was really three trailers joined longways, rested on top of three-foot-tall concrete supports. One rectangular floodlight shone pale from a fixture atop the middle section. It snowed steady now and the highway lanes beyond were rotten with white, but the plough hadn't passed in hours by the looks of it. Pa whistled loud by his thumb and forefinger. Not two seconds later a flashlight sparked from beside the trailer. Twice more. Pa took his sled down the grade into the clearing, pulled up on the forest side of the trailer. Uncle Dougie came out from the shadow and went over to talk to the big man. After a couple of seconds Pa waved us down. He got up from the sled and unlatched part of the tow trailer tarp and reached in. Came out with a portable acetylene torch rig, cylinders fixed inside a metal bracket, the hoses and torch nozzle pinned to the side of it. I walked over and took it. He went back under the tarp.

My Uncle Dan had gone out to watch the road, flashlight in hand. Ronnie was working the winch-straps loose and clearing the tarp from Dan's sled tow.

"Get this fucker next," Pa said to him, pointing at his own rig.

"Sure thing."

Pa looked over at me.

"Come with me, son," he said.

We walked around to the front of the place. Short stairwell leading to a metal security door, round knob on the right side with a deadbolt keyhole cylinder not far above it. There were windows in the front of the thing and they were aglow in the blues and reds of neon beer signs. The open sign was dark. Uncle Doug took his coat off and his snow pants, had a fire-proof jumpsuit on under his gear. He put a welding bucket on and gloved up. Pa stood there with a twelve-pound sledge dangling from his bearclaw by the handle. He looked back to the road and whistled again. The flashlight lit up and went dark twice.

"Get goin'," he said. "Quick to it."

Dougie went up the stairs with the torch rig and opened up the cylinder valves, oxygen first then the acetylene, opened up the acetylene control valve on the torch, lit it with the striker. Fierce yellow flame fired from the nozzle. He turned the oxygen valve on the torch handle and tempered that flame to a straight and even blue line. He started the cut high up around the deadbolt and doorknob. Then went to the hinges on the left of the thing. Sparks flew wild and lit tiny glow-fires in the wooden decking that Uncle Doug worked from. When he turned off the torch and cleared out there were angry red lines in the door.

"What d'ya think?" Pa said. "Will she go?"

Uncle Doug just took off the helmet and smiled at him.

"You and your fuckin' cousin better bring those trailered sleds around front," Pa said to me.

After that he stomped heavy up the stairs and wound up with the sledge, hit the door good and low. The whole thing shifted in from the framing and then started to topple outward.

THE WAY BACK HOME WAS LONG and cold and seemed like to never end, no matter the adrenaline and the whiskey we'd slung back before setting out, saddled low with case upon case of cargo. We ran in one line again and farther apart yet than we'd come. Snow fell hard around us, lonely world of ice and narrow lamp beams. Ronnie tried to hoot and hol-ler early on in the trip but it was lost on the wind. He was awful quiet by the time we saw the opposite shore. I tried to make out our earlier tracks but they were long gone and there would not be a trace of our night travels for anyone to see come morning. Even the bonfire that we lit later in our yard—fuelled with branded cardboard boxes, Styrofoam peanuts, plastic and packing tape—lay as but a volcano-holed mound when the sun came up to snowblind those poor working souls that rose with it.

BY LATE WINTER WE HAD GONE AS FAR AS Parry Sound for new quarry, and we'd come back and hit two of the same liquor stores again. Pa listened to the radio day and night and was often out watching the skies and the stars like they would tell him something secret about when and where to go next. In times of thaw he worked long hours on the sleds and bikes and his old Mercury. So was his claim to a legitimate mechanics business.

We ate a lot of dinners at Aunt Colette's and less and less did Ronnie provoke profanities out of my old man. Pa even took the guy out shooting and they brought home a ten-point buck with one side of its rack blown to pieces by Ronnie, a good deal of the meat ruined and lousy with buckshot. Pa cut what he could and sent it down the road to Aunt Colette. He would not let Ronnie keep the half-rack. He left it in my bed as a joke when he was drunk and I found it drunk and pitched it out into the woods while I was taking a piss off our back deck.

In the papers, they called us booze bandits. I had a chuckle at that and Pa never got tired of reading it. He would save me the clippings. After we robbed a trailer out in Port McCall, Pa had gone out for the paper bright and early and woke me up to read it. He'd drunk nearly all of a forty pounder of rye and hadn't slept a wink.

"You see our friend the chief got a statement in the fuckin' paper?"

"I do now," I said.

"Says he's lookin' at leads. All kinds of fuckin' leads he says."

"Yeah?"

"Then he says that they're lookin' for any information from citizens with any goddamn information."

"Yeah?"

"You know what that means, Charlie, you little shit?"

"Not yet."

"Means they ain't got no fuckin' goddamn leads."

WITH SPRING WE LOST THE ICE ON the lake and the trails in the woods and there went the business for the season. The sleds were stowed and stored and what little of the booze that hadn't been sold or shipped far was wrapped and buried in a grown-over gravel pit way back in the barrens. I took a job drivin' the delivery truck for the FoodTown, our one crap supermarket. Sometimes I took extra shifts stocking shelves. I had tried for a job in the next town over, with the golf courses and marinas, but that didn't pan out. When they saw my name they'd stiffen up and ask who my folks were. So I told them. That was about as far as I got before they quit listening and tried to hustle me out of the room.

I had a busted old pickup that Pa helped me get on the road. Bought from a local fella for three cases of good whiskey and the promise that if ever the origin of that whiskey was told to cops there'd be a house on fire in the foothills with the owner still inside. I drove that truck to work every morning and it looked like hell but ran like a champ. Hotter days settled in by June and I had to drive shirtless with the windows pinned down so as not to sweat through my work clothes before I got to the fucking supermarket.

By and by I met a girl who worked at the deli counter. Dirty blonde hair and blue eyes and an anklet tattoo. She still went to the high school I'd just come out of. She said I was once her peer tutor in biology, but I didn't remember her as she would've been but fourteen and didn't ever say a word back then. Her name was Claire. We got stuck working Saturday mornings sometimes and she looked prettier still for all her hangovers and ragged ponytails and tired eyes with no make-up. One such morning I'd come in late and had to go out behind the back of the place and puke my guts out all over the fresh-laid asphalt in the backlot. I came in for a hose to wash it down and when I was done she watched me curious as I swiped a travel-size bottle of mouthwash and walked back through the store to the bathroom at back.

At my lunch break I lay half-awake in the driver's seat of the truck, windshield blocked out by a cover that reflected the sunlight back out. It was still goddamned hot. I'd found a warm bottle of beer underneath the seat and had it in my hand with a ball cap over top. I took a drink and then looked out the window to make sure there wasn't anybody out there who'd dime me out. As I was scoping the place I heard the small shuffle of sneakers on the pavement but it didn't register.

"Hey," she said loud.

I near leapt out of my skin and grabbed hold of the wheel with my free hand. When I turned Claire was standing there in the passenger window, slender fingers on the window frame, pale blue eyes staring at me.

"Jesus fuckin' Christ," I said.

"Rough one today, huh?"

I shuffled in the seat and waved the beer around like I might find somewhere to put it.

"Can I have a sip?" she said.

"Warm as piss," I said.

"Lovely. But I'll give it a go."

Claire reached over and took the bottle from me and took a good pull. She didn't look around to check if anyone saw her. She handed the bottle back and I rested it on my leg. She had faint sweat marks on her shirt where her collarbones met, little wisps of hair stuck flat below her ears.

"When you workin' 'til?" she said.

"Three."

"You think you could give me a lift home?"

"Okay."

"Don't you need to ask where I live?"

"Where d'you live?"

She smiled.

"Just on the south side of town. Near the grain elevators."

"Alright."

"You live out in the harbour, right? You sure it ain't out of your way?"

"I'm not in no hurry to get back out there."

THROUGH THAT SUMMER I DROVE Claire home every shift we worked together. Never straight there. We often drove out to the pier-head at the far end of town, where the fishing was bad from the factories and thick treecover blocked you from the road. She kissed deep, fast-tongued. Sometimes so hard it hurt my top gums. I'd put my hand down her pants and try to work at an angle with the cab armrest in the way. Sometimes she'd let me figure things out myself by the way she moved and the sounds she made and how hard she took hold of my forearm when I got it right. Sometimes she'd tell me what to do and how and she wasn't shy about it. And when she climbed over and sat straggle-legged on me, hair hanging down at my ears, warm breath at my forehead as we tried to get the necessary garments off, I could barely stop my heart from beating a hole through my chest. Whether you called that feeling love or not I could still live off it for a good long time.

SUMMER STRETCHED LONG THAT YEAR. Too hot and dry enough to nearly rout bumper crops on farms at town's edge. Sunbaked soil under row upon row of stunted plant lines between concession roads. There was a fire ban on. Boats had their out-boards torn out in shallowed channels around the bay. When fall came at last it stayed but weeks and then cold rain started to fall. Colder and colder and the first snowfall early in October. Snowbanks two feet high aside the town roads while kids trudged brave through the white on Halloween, ghouls and goblins in winter boots. I went to work at the FoodTown still, hammering the heater with my palm when it stalled out. The truck never took more than two turns of the key to fire the engine. When I left in the mornings now, Pa was not in the garage at his cars and he wasn't in his bed sleeping it off. He was either down the road at Aunt Colette's and

Ronnie's or he was at the kitchen table in his skivvies, listening to the radio.

Me and Ronnie were sent to the scrappers, deep in the backcountry. I had to put chains on my truck tires. It took the whole day but we made it back around suppertime with a bed full of parts. At the house the sun set red through gaps in the wood, lit the frozen roadway in weird colours. Thick woodsmoke rose from the chimney cap, hanging like a fog. The garage door was open and Pa sat a deckchair at the head of the drive with a beer in his hand, the shop stereo spitting news and weather. He wore just his boots and coveralls, wool sweater underneath. Watched us come up like we were travelling salesmen.

"How'd we do?" he said.

"Got everythin' you told us to."

"Okay."

"He would've took a case less for it, but Ronnie piped up."

Pa's bottom lip curled so that his beard covered all of his mouth. He turned to where Ronnie stood in the garage, already at the shop-fridge with his hand on a bottle of beer. Ronnie straightened up and his mouth opened a little.

"Good," Pa said to Ronnie. "Good for you, son."

Ronnie nodded and cracked the beer. He couldn't help himself from smiling. I just shook my head. Pa turned to me.

"Why would ya pay a man less than he's owed if he's fair to trade with and a friend to fuckin' boot?"

"I wasn't tryin' to stiff the guy. Just tryin' to get us a better trade."

"Well, next time just follow Ronnie's lead and trade what yous are fuckin' told to trade. Alright?"

I was about to say something else but it just gave up halfway and came out as a puff of air over my lips. I went to the fridge and got a beer and Ronnie leaned up against the dropcloth of the Mercury. I thought he would catch a slap for that one but Pa barely bristled. I started for the garage stairs to the house and got as far as the first step.

"We got work to do startin' early tomorrow," Pa called to me over his shoulder.

"I'm at the FoodTown in the mornin'."

"Nope. You are retired."

"I can't just fuckin' not show up ever again."

He sat up and turned.

"You go there tomorrow an' I'll come in bare-assed and knock the teeth out your manager's head in front of all your buddies. And your pretty girl."

"Fuck," I said.

"Now both of you pull up a chair here with the old man. We got plenty to discuss before the mornin' comes."

WE HIT THE FIRST STORE TOWARD THE END of that month. Three in the morning with a portable halogen lamp shining eerie light from the underside of the trailer. Uncle Doug cut through the wooden baseboards with a jigsaw and pulled the insulation matting clear. Cut through the actual flooring and climbed inside. I went in after. We lowered boxes down through the opening onto long sleighs made from the hood metal of old cars. They were pulled clear and emptied and slid back until the tow trailers were half-sunk to the ground. Before we let out, Dougie got back under the store with a pair of two-by-fours and set the flooring again, bolted it in. He shovelled the insulation back into the gap and wedged the sawed base panel back before shimmying away.

The next four liquor trailers went staggered, two local stores with a few weeks between them. Then two stores at a three-hour ride to the northeast and three-hour ride back, and those robberies done but three days apart. We had to lug fuel so that we wouldn't have to stop. The cold near crippled us and some of the sleds struggled over the length. We did both of those jobs with Doug on the torch and when we got back from the second job he sat bone-chilled by our wood fire with his hands burnt and bruised. He had good whiskey and water in a tall glass and drank through a straw.

"Why in fuck did we do those two like that again?" he said.

Dad got out of his armchair and knelt by the fire. Took up his brother's hands in his own and kneaded the joint muscles, careful by the little stump.

"Two jobs in a row with that kind of gear to haul makes it look local."

"What?"

"Local to there, Dougie."

On the next job me and Ronnie went through the roadside windows of a store in the next county with a sledge and fire-axe. Made a godawful mess of the place. Ronnie cleared the framing with the axe and boosted me in, handed up the sledge. The alarms squealed loud enough to blow your eardrums. I carried the hammer to the front door and swung near the knob. Blew the hasp clear out from the jamb and let the door swing and come back. Ronnie came in and split the alarm siren with the axe and it warbled low and quit. We worked double-quick to load the booze and fire up the sleds. Tore through the bush to our home county but a half-hour away.

Constable Francis came by the house the next afternoon. He carried his girth around back to where my Pa shovelled a blackened slush heap into a wheelbarrow for me to haul. We could see the big man coming by his gait but he wore only jeans and flannel, a ball cap on his huge head. Pa stared at him for a second and then kept on shovelling.

"I can't remember when I last seen you outta your blues, Francis," Pa said.

"Sometimes I change outta them. For church and the like."

"It ain't Sunday."

"I hear Jesus saves any day of the goddamned week now."

Pa smiled. He planted the shovelhead in the muck.

"What the fuck's he doin'?" I said.

"Shut up," said Pa.

Francis studied me calmly from across the yard.

"Heard you got a job at the FoodTown?" he said to me.

"I did."

"You ain't got work today?"

"I quit."

"Oh?"

"He's helping me round the shop," Pa said.

Francis nodded.

"What is it you want exactly?" Pa said.

"I need to talk to ya, Rick."

"As a cop or as a regular person?"

Francis stood up tall as he could get and eyeballed my dad.

"Don't be a fool," he said.

Pa stared at Francis a long time. Then he handed me the shovel and said he'd be back. They left out together in Francis' car and they were gone for hours.

BY NIGHTFALL THE OLD MAN WAS back and full of whiskey, stink of bar-room sweat in his clothes. He sat heavy at the kitchen table and fumbled with the radio. Those massive fingers gently turning the dials. He had not uttered more than a grunt.

"He knows, don't he?" I said.

Pa grumbled, took a drink.

"The cops got nothin'. 'Bewildered' is how he put it. But they're ready to start casting out in any direction just out of pure fuckin' embarrassment."

"What's that mean?"

"You see any cars parked in the road of a night, you let me know."

I PICKED CLAIRE UP FROM HER HOUSE. She had her hair teased out and let down and wore jeans and a girl's golf shirt. Little make-up to colour her pale cheeks, faintest eye-shadow. She hustled out to the truck and tried to put her jacket on as she went.

When she got in she kissed me long and tasted like wine and bubblegum.

Aunt Colette had roast chicken and potatoes ready in the oven when we got there. I led Claire in through the side door where the yard-bound mutt licked at her hand. Colette peeked over from the stove when we came in. Red-haired and tall with thick, strong arms. Slippered feet on the linoleum.

"Charlie, you are late," she said.

"Sorry Aunt Col."

She studied the both of us. Took a long look at Claire. She smiled and cocked a thumb toward the sitting room.

"Animals are in back," she said, eyes on Claire yet. "Honey. You can stay here with me."

Claire took to all of them like nothing. She talked to Aunt Colette about what it was like in the high schools now and she talked to Ronnie about her older sister, Karen. Ronnie said Karen probably wouldn't remember him but Claire said she did. She talked to her last week. The sister lived out west now. Ronnie nodded solemn but he got a charge out of the whole thing. Pestered Claire throughout the meal. Pa said little until he was done eating. He waited for us all to finish and took all the plates to the kitchen. Came back with a good bottle of whiskey and set it by the wine on the table. Pa poured a glass and slid it down to Ronnie. Then he leaned in toward Claire.

"This here Irish wine is better than the girly stuff sittin' there," he said. "Don't know if you got the taste for it."

"I could have a small one," Claire said.

Pa poured the glass quarter-full without looking at it. Claire took it and Colette squinted her eyes at the girl, looked down at her placemat for a second. Pa sent me a half-glass and poured his glass full to the brim.

"To Claire," he said, raising the thing thimble-like between his thumb and forefinger. "May her luck with men improve by the day."

Ronnie busted out laughing until I backhanded him at the shoulder. We all drank. Claire downed the stuff in one slow gulp and set the glass down. Not a twitch or shudder. Pa smiled a little.

"What's your dad do for a livin', Claire?" he said.

"He works at the TRW. Runs the floor for the morning shift."

Dad nodded.

"What'd he say when you told him you were comin' out for dinner?"

"Try to be back by midnight."

"Yous aren't from here, originally?" he said.

Claire shifted, ran her hair back behind her ear.

"Moved here when I was ten. Dad is from Rochester and my mom's from Niagara Falls."

My Pa poured himself another whiskey. Tipped another small one into Claire's glass. He winked at her.

"She's a good'un, son," he said.

CLAIRE HELPED AUNT COLETTE with the dishes for a few minutes until Col told her to grab me and get along. I got up from the couch and gave Ronnie the finger. He tried to swat it out of the air. Pa sat heavy in an armchair and he saluted lazily at me as I went.

Barely did he look up. We left the house and my aunt watched us by the lamplight at the side door. Claire kept looking back and waving. My aunt held a hand up.

The truck rumbled heavy on snowed-over ruts in the forest lane. Pine branches whapped along the edges of the windshield and brushed the length of the truck. Out we came into a clearing, the ground under two feet of snow. Nothing there but the hoof prints of a wayward deer, twinned rabbit tracks. I pulled up crooked on a shieldrock plateau that fell five feet to frozen water. To the right stood a set of falls that spilled yet and broke thin-formed slates of ice over and over. There was a six-pack of tallboys by Claire's feet. She pulled one and popped the tab, took a drink. She saw that the armrest at the bench-middle had been taken out, moorings and all. Then she handed the can over to me and pulled her shirt up over her head.

Not too long afterward we lay there on the bench with the windows all afog. There was little room to move and I'd had to shift toward the dash, thighs pressed up against the steering wheel and my ass halfway off the seat cushion. The heater had gone again but nobody noticed until our breath started to hang in the air. I bashed the console once with the underside of my fist and the fans whirred.

Claire shuffled her elbows along my chest until she had propped herself up there, eyes fixed on a fat collarbone scar I'd earned at five years old. I felt the curve of her back with the rough flat of my hand. Asked her what was the matter.

"We gotta be more careful," she said.

"Okay."

"I'm on the pill. But I'd rather be paranoid than barefoot and pregnant at seventeen."

"I hear ya," I said.

"You can never tell what might happen. Just look at your aunt."

My mouth opened to talk and then it shut up. I started to breathe so hard that the girl rose and fell a good four inches atop me. Claire looked into my eyes and took hold of my head firm with both hands.

"My God, Charlie," she said soft. "Didn't you know it?"

OUT IN THE YARD I STOOD WITH a bottle of whiskey upended and fixed to my lips. I drank deep and near had to take a knee before drinking again. Then I pitched the bottle at the house. It glanced off the siding and emptied on the narrow back porch, spinning oddly. I went up the steps and put a barbeque lighter to the spilt booze but it wouldn't take. I opened the back door and walked in.

Pa had settled into his armchair with a short glass in his hand and a few bottles of beer on the nearby side table. Otherwise, the house was immaculate. He looked up at me for just a second and then went back to watching the TV. I stooped down next to the fireplace, lifted a fifty-pound ceramic plant pot, soil and tree and all. I trod over and dropped it through the living room table. Dirt and debris flew as the wooden tabletop slammed down to the carpet. Pa got to his feet and I stepped over the mess and drove him back against the wall with my shoulder. We careened off the panelling and went over the chair and then we were rolling on the carpet. Scrambling to our feet in front of the TV. He had me by the collar and cuffed me hard with an open hand. The weight of it stung me but I was at him again until he pitched backward and took out an entire length of shelving with our old pictures and postcards and framed letters from wars past, pages yellowed.

In the centre of the room he stood tall, wheezing, hands half up. He could've killed me and we both knew it. I lunged and caught him on the jaw with an overhand right. Back and back he stepped, arms reaching while the walls came down around him. He did not fall. I saw him duck and bolt and then I was up by the ceiling fan, down on the floorboards with my guts afire and not a breath left in me. I swatted at his great and ugly face until he held my wrists.

"Calm down, son," he said.

We could have been minutes like that, or hours.

MILD WEATHER SETTLED IN THROUGH late winter. The roads were clear for many weeks and snow lay but sparse on lawns and farm fields. Unlucky fishermen had their huts founder and collapse on the ice, or they came by of a morning to see a jagged, slush-filled hole and no more. Pa spent his days at Aunt Colette's and watched the round of her belly grow. He drank plenty and it never appeared that he'd slept. Ronnie didn't seem to know how to talk to me but the sentiment I got from him was just goddamned overwhelming joy. Like if we weren't brothers before I had no choice now. Dummy. Like we weren't before.

At the tail end of March we got one good cold snap, an Alberta clipper they called it, minus thirties in the day and bone-chillers overnight. Pa and his brothers were in the garage late hours and I started waking to fry-ups in the kitchen. Two platters at our little, barewood table. The old man would watch out of the corner of his eye to see if I'd eat or not. I did.

One morning Pa quit eating and put his elbows on the tabletop, wrapped one busted hand with the other and looked at me.

"We're gonna take another run."

"Ice ain't thick enough," I said.

"This cold'll last another week. After that, season's up. We gotta go."

"When?"

"Early Sunday mornin'."

"The ice ain't thick enough."

He just shrugged and went back to his breakfast. I wolfed what I could in the five minutes I could stand to sit there and then I cleaned the plate and set it by the sink. Got my coat and hat and went out the front door, down to the truck with my boots unlaced. I drove the length of our street with my teeth rattling in my head. I'd done laps of dirt road by the time the heat kicked in. I parked atop a rise just north of us and from there I could see clear to Aunt Colette's house.

OF COURSE I WENT WITH MY PA for that run in the bitter fucking cold. We set out to rob a trailer at county's edge, a triple-jointed sucker again and we went in messy, no need for the torch or the industrial saws. It snowed light and stopped while we scooped out the cargo. I did not like that. Pa had planned for it. Ronnie helped breach the place and then he took off on Dan's loaded-up cargo sled, following the shoreline as close as he could, where the ice was thicker by inches. At a paved launch near to the far shoreline a U-Haul sat with a box big enough to carry the two cargo sleds, a ramp that lowered to the ground. The other sleds would ride long trails and switchbacks and cut across lengths of county road, down dirt paths where the frozen claypack would take no marks.

By the time we got the second tow trailer loaded Dan was already pegging it across the frontlot, screaming bloody murder, but we couldn't make it out. Before he made it over we could hear the sirens. Faint as a whistling breeze but getting louder by the second. Pa mounted his sled and rode up over the trailhead lip, careful until he made it onto the trail proper. All of the gear and booze went with him into the dark. Dan and Doug followed and I brought up the rear and stopped just inside the path, got off my sled and used a length of busted plywood to shovel over the snow at the trail gap. I threw it sidelong into the woods and hopped onto my sled. Gunned it for the bay.

I seen my uncles ahead like two cat's eyes, my own headlamp shining at their back reflectors. They got bigger and bigger. I tried to look back to shore but I was going like a rocket and couldn't bring myself to turn entire. The near naked ice played hell on the sled skis and my arms were already bone-sore. I held the handlebars as hard as I could. Up ahead, the two lead sleds were bigger yet and then one of them took a cut to the side and it was off the goddamn surface, swelling and narrowing in size and casting light like a flashlight thrown and spiralling. Then all I could see was the brake lights of the other sled and a round circle of shadow atop the ice that took shape awful quick as I closed on it.

My Uncle Doug lay sideways on the ice with his arms pinned between his thighs, like he had to take a piss. His right leg had been turned at an impossible angle and was too long by inches. I got off the sled and slid over on my knees. His helmet had a nasty gouge out of it and the visor was gone. I shook him and could see his eyelids twitch by the headlamp light that spilled over us. Uncle Dan had wheeled around and now he pulled up and got off his sled. For a second he just stood there with his helmet in his hand. Then he dragged me up by my armpit, turned me to where we'd come from. Far out in the black there were lines of blue light shifting every which way.

"Go on, Charlie," he said. "I'll carry him. Tell your Pa what happened."

Not a half-mile gone, I came upon my Pa, standing on the ice beside his idling sled. He held his hand up for me to stop, about twenty feet out. He had his helmet off and his facemask at his neck. Frost clung to his beard. His one arm hung low at his backside and I could see the shotgun steel behind the leg. When he saw it was only me he set the gun down on the seat of his sled and came over by long strides.

"Where's the boys?" Pa said.

"Doug's sled caught a rut in the ice, threw him."

"Jesus."

"He was out when I left 'em. Uncle Dan told me to go on. Said they'd be along directly."

The big man turned and hustled to his sled. He came back with the shotgun and had me hold it while he fixed his mask and put his bucket on, opened the visor. He stared at me. Took the gun.

"Get up, son," he said.

I cleared off of my machine.

"Head for the shore on my sled. When you get there don't you wait on us. Ronnie'll want to wait but you knock him out if you got to and drive on."

"Dad."

"Do not go home 'til I come for ya."

He settled heavy on my sled and took off, circled wide and started back across the ice. The skies had cleared and a sliver of moon shone meagre above us. Tiny lamplight at either shore where people had cut their homes. Treetop shadows like thousands of bottom-row teeth. Pa but a scrap in the white as he sped away.

We waited as long as we could, but then we did go home. By the pale daybreak. On foot and frozen through to the bone, shuffling side by side through the thick of the wood. Ronnie couldn't keep it up so we found the sled trail and walked the old, ice-hardened tracks. At the back fringe of my yard we crouched behind trees and watched the sun come up, scouted the place and saw not a sign of life.

The fire would not burn high enough for Ronnie. He kept feeding it until the flames choked and all but died. I ran a near-hot bath and made him get in it. Told him to get used to it before filling it hotter. I gripped his hand like men do, thumb locked to thumb. Then I left him there with a half-bottle of whiskey, the base of it underwater and pinned to his middle with both hands. I sat in the living room armchair in my underpants with four layers of blankets over my chapped hide. Whiskey and beer at the side table. I had the house phone and a CB radio within arm's reach.

No call ever came because my dad and his brothers went through the ice that Sunday in March, one brother perhaps dead already but we would never know for sure. They fell under the weight of their sleds and went down to the black and were not retrieved until late the next day, stropping the underside of a thin sheet of ice near the eastern shoreline. They had all bunched and froze together like mussels. Had to be chipped apart with a hammer and chisel in the hospital ambulance bay before they were brought to the morgue, so as not to unsettle the podunk doctors and orderlies. At least that's how it's told in town.

Further told as myth and legend are all the accounts of people who sat at the Anchor Tavern the day before Pa and his brothers were buried. Police Chief Donald Moreau had just come off a news show where he talked all about the outlaws he ran down and who sadly fell victim to their own hubris that cold fucking night. Way he told it was the cops tried to throw lines to the three men when the ice gave out. Could not save them. But the chief didn't know, and nor did I, that Ronnie went to the site where my Pa and uncles fell in the black of night and he crawled to the hole belly-down. Found buckshot in the gnawed up brink, same gauge that might be fired from a standard police scattergun. And Ronnie had those pellets in his jacket pocket when he came into the Anchor, rancid from

Pa's wake, and blew a quarter of the police chief's head off with a sawed-off .22 rifle.

There are quiet days now. Calm days and I wake up most mornings cold in my bed. In a very clean house that has long been paid for and runs little hydro and commands next to nothing in property tax to the county. I don't see many visitors. The old cop Francis came out once to tell me he wasn't at the lake. That he was sorry about my Pa. I didn't let him past the foot of the drive. I hear he's since retired. I been trying my best to keep a real garage running out of the place and I often set to work on the old Mercury coupe. Even ran it without plates or insurance through the backroads with a pretty young girl under my arm. Just the once, or twice. I spend as much time as I can at my Aunt Colette's house, trying to help her when she'll let me. Round as she is and fit to burst, she still won't let me stay long. Claire goes there often and sometimes she stays late into the night, talking about possible futures. Colleges that could be. Babies that will be. Lonely homes with just one person in each, how to make them full.

If Claire comes over of a night from my aunt's, we curl up and play house. I drink a lot and she drinks less and less. She always falls asleep before I do and that is when I miss my mother and father. Talk to them long in the thinnest hours of the night. Drunk and damned and waiting for the answers, a girl's head by my heart that by God scares me more than the quiet.

ONE WE COULD STAND TO LOSE

ARTHUR WALKED THE LOBBY OF the hotel in his suit-trousers and stopped by framed photographs of the place lit in gold and silver light, black limousines waiting the length of that city block. Behind one picture there was a faint stain from a blast of blood and vomit and he knew it because he'd fixed the frame over that ruined patch of wallpaper. He knew the layout of each floor and what rooms were hired and what rooms were condemned and bolted shut. Arthur walked to the office and relieved a young lady with black, black hair and a bullring in her nose. She took her things and left without a word. He sat behind the desk and slid the window open. Sound of thunder from below. Nightclub that ran all hours underneath the hotel. Arthur felt it by the soles of his shoes.

A tall Jamaican man came through the front doors in a tank top. He sidled up to the front desk. Sweaty skin of his arms and neck. Eyes red and sunken.

"Arthur, my man," the Jamaican said.

"Hi, Ollie. How many?"

The man dropped a ten-dollar bill on the counter and Arthur took it, ducked low. He spun the dial to a safe built into the floor under the desk. He came back with two mason jars of still whiskey and slid them over to the Jamaican.

"Whoo," the man said.

"That'll put some hair on your chest," Arthur told him.

The man bagged the jars and walked through the lobby, waved as he left by the streetside doubledoors. Panes gone foggy with grit and glass-splattered insects.

IN THE EARLY MORNING ARTHUR heard two drunks screaming at each other through the plaster walls. One woman called another woman a cocksucker. He turned his radio on and sat on his mattress. The bed linens were clean because Arthur bought them long ago and laundered them himself. He had torn up his carpeting near the turn of the century and carted it down to the alleyway dumpster piece by piece. When Arthur got up to piss at night he walked barefoot on creaky hardwood, and he often sat in his chair barefoot and read late with his feet on the cedar planking.

He'd not slept long when someone knocked his door. By the clock it was eleven a.m. Arthur got up and went over to see by the peephole. He opened up on a frantic clerk who worked the morning shift. The man was near dancing on the hallway carpet. Eyes agog and his face gone red.

"What is it, Tim?"

"It's goddamn chaos down there. They come in through the front door and then came some more and they just started goin' at it."

"Who did?"

"Most of 'em ran. But the dude from two-sixteen is face-down in the lobby with all kinds of stuff comin' outta him."

ARTHUR CLEARED OUT A SMALL AND stumbling crowd to better look at the downed man. He'd ended up mouth to carpetfabric and blew laboured breaths into a little pool of his own blood and upchuck. Arthur tried to speak to the man but he wasn't conscious. The cops and ambulance had long been called and Arthur set the man into the recovery position and held the man's sweaty head in both hands. The man trembled steady like a current had been run through him.

The paramedics took the man out on a gurney with a tube down his throat. He had his eyes closed and a bubble of mucus and plasma swelling at the corner of his mouth. Arthur stood beside the morning clerk as he tried to spit out his story to the cops. Then Arthur spoke to them awhile and to the smattering of firemen and paramedics that kept on in the lobby.

"You fellas always come in pistols drawn for an injury like that?"

The one cop shrugged.

"We ever answer a disturbance call here we come in pistols up, period."

HE TENDED THE WHISKEY STILL IN AN old boiler room below the hotel proper. The elevator and stairwell went down to a sub-basement that only he and the building owner could access by master key. Nobody but Arthur had been down there for years. He spent many of his off hours in that room with its centenary bricks chipped and sweating. He wore his undershirt over his small belly, forearms thick with cord-muscle, old merchant navy tattoos about his shoulders and biceps. No matter the time of day or night he felt basstones through the heavy stone. Liquids rippled where they were flasked and bottled. He'd come to not mind it.

By bulblight he worked and checked his watch. Half-hour until his night shift at the counter. He took up a crate of jars packed in newspaper and cardboard egg-cartons. On his way out he flicked the light switch with his elbowbone, hefted the crate with just his right arm as he closed the boiler room door.

THE BLACK-HAIRED GIRL SPUN IN HER chair when Arthur came in. She had a tiny ceramic bone through the centre-hole in her nose now. Skin around her eyes dark with make-up, drawn to a point toward her ears. She stared at him and he just went about signing in and checking the booth. He'd set a canvas bag on the counter with another half-dozen jars in it.

"Can I have one?" she said.

"If you got five dollars."

She dug in her pocket and held out a crumpled bill. He looked at her then.

"Sweet Jesus," he said.

"Think it's too much?"

"What you mean?"

She flicked the nosebone.

"Oh that," he said. "I didn't even notice. I was just overwhelmed a minute by the smell of whatever hippie concoction they sold you for armpit deodorant."

She smiled white, white teeth. Dentist since childhood teeth. He handed her a jar and pocketed the five. She put the jar in her purse but didn't leave.

"Want to have a drink with me? Gotta pass some time before I meet a friend."

"I'll have a sit with ya. Just keep that low in case somebody comes in."

The girl set up on a low stool in the front corner of the office, just her head showing over the countertop. Took the jar out again and uncapped it.

"Tim told me you helped save a guy the other day."

"Don't know about that."

"How many people you seen get hurt in here?"

"More'n I'd like to say."

The girl sipped at the jar. Tilted her head back and breathed hot through her mouth. Kept it open.

"Holy shit," she said.

Arthur grinned.

"Are those old black and whites on the wall legit? With all the fancy limos and movie stars and shit?"

"Yep. Was a nice place."

"What happened?"

"I don't know. What ever does happen? It was for a long time and then it wasn't."

The girl's pants-pocket started to sing and she slumped to pinch out her cellphone. She looked at it and stood up. Capped the whiskey jar and put it inside her purse again.

"You gonna tell me about what I first asked?" she said.

Arthur had his palm against his cheek and the elbow of that arm on the counter. He used it to turn on the stool.

"I'd already lived in the hotel for three years when I found the first body. Some Indian fella. Pock-scarred face. No shirt on. An' he was slumped over dead in the elevator car. Had a buck-knife buried in his chest to the hilt. That body left in a plastic bag and the carpet it bled all over was torn up and replaced. I figure by 'bout ninety-four I seen five more bodies leave the building on hand-stretchers or gurneys. I didn't find none of those but I knew two of 'em by name."

The girl looked like she might smile but couldn't get her cheeks to do the work. Arthur stared at her plainly.

"I'd better go," she said. And so she did.

ON HIS NIGHT OFF ARTHUR WENT next door to the adjoining blues bar. That place still jumped if they got the right band in there. Arthur drank a ginger ale and watched a triple of young men hammer their way through a blues-rock set. There were neon lights hung around the place on the exposed brick and hardwood walls. They'd re-upholstered the booths and benches and had weatherproofing done on the windows and roofshingles. That stage kept on drawing blood and guts players from all over the map. Not a one stayed in the hotel.

The bartender topped up Arthur's drink and wiped down the patch of bar top that the old man held. He stayed there awhile and let the other servers take customers.

"You hear that the O'Flynn boy is gonna sell?"

"Come again."

"Got papers filed with the city, proposals about knocking your place down and turnin' most of the block into student housing. They says they don't plan to flatten the bar but it'll go too, I'm sure of it."

Arthur scratched at his head and heard but didn't hear the band. He stared long at the barman.

"Arthur," the barman said. "You still with me?"

"Ain't no way," he said.

The barman shrugged, shouldered his towel and rested heavy against the bar. "That true you signed a hundred-year lease to rent your spot?" he said.

"Somethin' like that, but it don't matter."

"They gotta honour it."

"Well, the old man is long gone. An' I suppose I can't lease the room if they knock down the buildin'."

"What'll you do?"

"The boy O'Flynn had those tenements up north that turned slum. That's well known. So, I guess I'll just keep goin' to work and hope that the city tells him where to stick his plans."

NEAR SHIFT'S END ARTHUR STARTED head-nodding at the desk. He was looking at an empty lobby then he was looking at nothing. Then he was looking at the lobby again with a giant drunk called Papamanolis pinwheeling around the place, casting about every which way.

"Good God man," Arthur said. "What are ye doin'?"

The man sidestepped twice to his right and then stopped. Looked like he might list that way but he came back straight like a wind-bent pine finally let alone. Papamanolis stood about six-foot-eight and his head was built right into his shoulders. He'd a barrel chest and beer gut but his gorilla-muscle arms had held their ridges and rises, blue weld-burn scars spread out over the skin from wrist to shoulder. The man studied Arthur from across the lobby.

"I gotta find Rosa," he said.

"She ain't here. You can leave a message with me if you want."

"I'm goin' up."

"You're bloody well not."

Papamanolis wobbled once and then he bolted for the stairs. Went up three steps at a time with one huge hand on the banister and the other flat to the wallpaper. Arthur got on the horn with the cops and told them the necessaries. Then he came out from behind the desk, locked the booth and made for the staircase.

The giant had already put his right arm through the door and he was stuck there to the shoulder. Shrieking from inside the room. Sound of metal being rung. Papamanolis managed to pull his arm free and take a step back. An iron skillet flew from the hole and glanced off the huge man's elbow, took another angle and went down to the hallway carpeting like a shot fowl. Papamanolis had his arm back in the hole again by the time Arthur got to the last turn in the staircase. The door bowed with the man against it and reaching blindly for the deadbolt inside. Arthur sucked wind and hustled up the last few steps, turned and measured the giant up. He swung the shillelagh against the big man's right knee and Papamanolis sagged to that side, arm pinned yet in the door. He'd started to roar when Arthur came back the other way and hit him by the temple. The giant dropped and he was limbstretched and gurgling when he carried over the stairwell lip and thumped down to the uppermost landing.

THE PARAMEDICS SPENT ABOUT TEN minutes trying to figure out how to get the man out of the stairwell. Finally they got him to come around, hair matted with blood and his shirtcloth soaked maroon in places. He ended up being more trouble conscious so they sedated him and ran him down the stairs using the gurney as a sled. It took six of them to get him into the ambulance hold.

"He took quite a wallop 'fore he went down, I imagine," the cop said.

"Couldn't say," Arthur said.

"He was down when you got up there?"

"Figure that skillet did the trick. Thrown with enough mustard on it."

The cop nodded.

"The lady. She won't press charges. Doesn't know she doesn't have to. He'll go away for this, record he has."

Arthur shrugged. The cop left him and started clearing the scene of other officers and fireman. When the cop came past to the streetside doors Arthur was standing there with a bucket of hot bleachwater. He waited a minute and then he started hauling it up the stairs.

THE FREE CITY PAPER WAS SITTING on the counter one night when Arthur spelled off the black-haired clerk again. He asked her if she wanted to buy more whiskey.

"Fuck no," she said, and left pretending to gag.

Arthur laughed and watched her go out into the humid dusk, fog of gnats hassling her as she went. Noise of the street and then the doors came back and sealed him in with the quiet. He set up at his post and then he read the paper, came to a page that had been deliberately dog-eared. He unfolded the flap and tried to work the crease with his palmheel. "Hard Luck Hotel" in masthead lettering. A newsprint photo of the very building where he sat reading. It took him a minute to recognize it, so little did he spend his time on the sidewalk looking at the building facade. Plans were relayed by the journalist, to level the place and build atop the plot. The article talked about pre-war glories for a paragraph and then told the crimes and murders and oddities for three. The O'Flynn boy was mentioned in there as were his failures and fibs. The historian they had interviewed about the hotel spoke to the little attention the hotel had gotten compared to other heritage buildings in the city, was asked to posit reasons why. "This is probably one we could stand to lose," he'd said.

Arthur leaned back on his stool and studied the lobby through the Plexiglas. Faint sound of doors opening and closing. Great ceiling fans moving re-circulated air. A young Dutchman came down by the stairs carrying a basket of dirtied work clothes, went toward the laundry room. Tall and sharp-shouldered with hair the colour of straw. When he came back he held one hand up with the littlest finger but a nub. Arthur smiled and the young man walked past the booth and went out the front doors into the black.

Arthur pulled a drawer and found the hotel ledger, opened it and looked to the inside front cover. He dragged the phone across the desk and picked up the receiver. Underscored the number with his forefinger as he dialed. On the eighth ring someone picked up.

"What is it?"

"I didn't wake you did I?"

"Arthur?" said O'Flynn.

"We need to talk, kid."

CONTRACTORS VISITED THROUGHOUT the fall and winter. If rooms went vacant they were closed for good and their keys were pulled from the office pegboard. By early spring O'Flynn stopped in at least once a week with city officials, tracked slush and roadgrit across the lobby flooring. Fixtures came down. The cherry wood stairwell railing was dismantled and wrapped in cloth. A high-hung chandelier built through with spider web cities had to be lowered and stripped and cleaned. The clerks were let go one by one until Arthur and the black-haired girl had to split the day between them in twelve-hour stands.

A nearby shelter found low-income housing for the lingering tenants and the black-haired clerk left with the last of them, crate of whiskey under her arm. Arthur missed her something terrible and he hadn't been prepared to feel like that.

O'Flynn had bought out Arthur's lease for six months' rent and whatever he could carry out of the place. Engineers were marking the walls and drilling holes for their charges during the end of his stay. Arthur could not really sleep nights so he rode an abandoned bicycle around the maze of hallways. When he did sleep he slept shallow and had odd dreams. Just a touch off the mark. The city perhaps a decade after the war. Arthur walking the centrevein main street from highway to lakeshore and casting out east and west from there. He wore a greycloth suit and his tiny nest-egg built into the brim of his hat. In the dream he was very tired and trod strangely. Next he was taking whiskey and beer in a dive bar near the university grounds. The real O'Flynn with his huge hands and head. Something wrong with his eyes. Arthur sat with a contract in his pocket and kept trying to call the barman. Above the backbar pictures of a woman and small boy in frames. He'd thought them lost and climbed over the bar to take them down.

He woke up slapping at his hindquarters where his back trouser-pocket should be. He turned over and found his wallet on the nightstand. Arthur looked at it for a time and then the cobwebs cleared. The wallet he'd been looking for was lost in a fire near forty years ago and the photographs went with it. He'd no address to send for more and no more letters were sent to him though he waited long for them and knew they'd never come.

ARTHUR LEFT THE HOTEL FOR THE LAST time on a Sunday morning. He took nothing but a small case of clothes and his other personals. Most of the rooms were still furnished with the windows curtained and the dusty bed linens rumpled atop their mattresses. Many of the doors were unlocked or open. O'Flynn was there to seal the building and trade Arthur his settlement for the hotel masterkeys. Arthur shook the man's hand and gave them up. O'Flynn did not check them.

TWO DAYS LATER ARTHUR CAME BACK into the hotel by the alley-bound sub-basement entry, travelled a series of broken steps and a long, damp corridor until he found the boiler room's back door. He'd come with a prybar and had to lever the thing open. All of his weight and gumption against the seized and oxidized hinge-bolts. He made space enough to shimmy through and then hauled the door shut behind him.

In his room he sat barefoot in the chair and listened to records. He'd taken his wristwatch off and laid it face up on the near side table. Three mason jars of whiskey stood aside it. At midnight he took his first drink in thirty-three years. He kept pace by the watch and counted minutes between each tilt of the jar. He sobbed but once and it didn't last. Fire blew in Arthur's nostrils from the second pint of whiskey. Dawn came gradual by the southeastern window, through part-drawn curtaincloth. By his footsoles he felt the first charges go. The empty jars slid across the tabletop. He sat alone and saw the world around him shift like water sloshing in a bucket.

SPREAD LOW ON THE FIELDS

S EAN O'HARA STOOD IN the hallway of his apartment while the phone told him that his old man was dead. He put his forearm to the wall and leant hard on it. The wallpanelling spoke a little under his weight. Otherwise the place was quiet as could be.

"Was it his heart?"

"I don't know any real way to tell you."

"What?"

"He was killed."

O'Hara looked at the receiver for a long time and then put it back at his ear.

"I don't know what you mean."

"There was an incident involving another resident here. Friend of his."

O'Hara had already gone back to his bedroom and he was into the drawers. The voice on the phone started up again but he cut it off.

"I live in the city," he said. "I'll be there before sun-up."

After that he pitched the phone sidelong across the room and heard the pieces dance across the flooring.

THEY CARRIED THE OLD MAN OUT on a gurney and O'Hara was there to watch him clear the ambulance doors. They'd not let him see the body and he had a mind to step up and pull back the sheet but the thought soured in his head right away. He sat aside with police in the front lobby of the retirement home until doors started opening and old, ponderous faces showed in the gaps, eyes blinking, one lady full awake and her hair bang-upright like she'd took lightning and lived. The cops asked him to follow them to the station to talk it over. They stood up but he didn't.

"Where's the fella that killed him?" O'Hara said.

"In his room with some other officers," said an older cop, tall and broad with hands you might find on a gorilla.

"He's not in holding?"

"Son," the cop said. "He don't even know he done it."

PERHAPS A DOZEN PEOPLE ATTENDED the funeral mass and Sean knew them all and talked long to some. He tried to draw up faces in his mind of folks who hadn't come by, but then he'd not been back to that town more than four times in ten years and didn't know who was truant or who was simply dead. An old friend who'd once cleared sawn-down pine acres by horse and cart with his father eulogized the man and it was short. Sean learned nothing new from anyone he talked to after the mass. He never saw any of them again.

In days to come he did not leave town. He dug in at a one-level motel that looked downhill to a land-locked and geese-shitted lake and he kept standing empty whiskey bottles and empty beer bottles on the counters and tabletops. Often he sat out front and watched leaves detach by the dozen and float away from the treeline. He'd already taken days off of work and he called back to the city site-office where he was foreman to say they should assume he'd need all of the days he had left for the year, even if it didn't turn out so. He slept nearly twenty-four hours in one stretch and woke up skullhammered at six-thirty of some morning and dragged ass to his car.

HE LEFT TOWN TO THE NORTH AND travelled a wooden bridge over patchwork swampland. The car struggled up a series of narrow foothill lanes with near hairpin switchbacks. The sun had cleared the eastern horizon and set columns of fire between the roadside pines. O'Hara had the windows open full and papers blew about at his feet. Woodsmoke in the air as he came upon a boarded filling station and soon afterward the busted main strip of the hillbilly hamlet. The last building he saw on that street sold fireworks and ammunition. A car sat crooked in the frontlot and a man seemed to be asleep in it. The store windows were dark yet.

He drove the little village in a wander, passing back through the centre street time and time again from the top and bottom side. He saw a diner open at one corner and slowed but thought better about stopping anywhere. Fifteen minutes gone he idled under a street sign and turned his hand over. Name of the road on his palm in black marker. O'Hara turned and crept the street with his head swivelling to either side like a lawnsprinkler. Some of the houses were not numbered but they were few enough to make the math easy.

ON THE TRIP BACK ACROSS THE marshway pass he didn't even feel part-drunk anymore and he lamented the hour of day and how much of it was left. O'Hara gave his head a shake and pulled into a greasy spoon at the reaches of town and went inside. Three old men sat with their cups. One at the counter. Two in booths. All of them apart. The waitress sat on the customer side of the counter in her smocks and she had her chin down at the crook of her elbow. She saw him come in by the backbar mirror and stood up slow.

He ate eggs and bacon, too much of it and too fast. Drank Coke instead of coffee and that got him a funny look from the waitress that lasted the whole time he was there. O'Hara read the city paper throughout the meal and when he got tired of it he shoved it aside and saw the town paper holstered in the napkin rack. He pulled it and laid the pages out and stopped chewing all at once.

They had a picture of his old man on the front. In the photograph, the elder O'Hara might have been fifty or so and he stood in the forefront of a bayside grain elevator. They'd cropped it mostly to his rockjaw face with all his scars and that bridgebroke nose. The photo wasn't much bigger than the kind you'd see in a passport. And beside it a grand, near full-page shot of the man that had killed him. His name was Charles DeCarlo Jr. and Sean knew that much but he'd not had a face to pair it with. Now he did. Younger days with a million-dollar smile and an army uniform hung with decorations. Infantryman in Korea wounded four times and discharged honourably with battle commendations at Kapyong and Seoul. Testimonials in there from family and friends as to his kindliness and gentle nature despite the many men he supposedly buried in the Far East. They reported him sequestered for good in the facility where he'd done for the elder O'Hara, stage six dementia that rendered him unfit to try at court. They'd lately moved him to another wing.

NOT A MILE FROM THE MOTEL HE sat at a stop sign for too long until he heard knocking at his window-glass. O'Hara turned quick to his left and saw a dark-haired woman aside the driver door. She held her hands out like he'd kept her waiting forever. He put the window down. She leaned in.

"Jesus," he said.

"Hi."

"How are you?"

She smiled at him. Little crow's feet by her eyes and her face slightly bigger, her hips rounder. She had rogue greys in her long and black, black hair. He couldn't slow the goings on in his chest and he didn't much try.

"How about we get out of the street?" she said.

O'Hara nodded.

"Where you headed?"

"Motel by the lake."

"Sweet Jesus, Sean," she said.

He watched her walk back to her truck, idling in the lane behind his car. She got in and shut her door. Nobody else in the road. He rolled out slow with the woman trailing him.

THEY SAT OUT ON THE PORCH in front of his room. Sean had an icechest at his feet full with bottles. He dragged it over so that it sat between their lawn-chairs. She didn't look at it, just at him and then at the motel grounds. He opened the chest and knuck-led two beers up from the icewater. He turned the caps one by one and offered her a bottle. She did not move for it. O'Hara drank one down to the dregs and set it by. Started on the other. She shook her head and took it out of his hand. Pulled deep and rested it on her chairarm. He dug another out and pulled the cap.

"I can only have the one," she said. "They're waitin' at home for someone to feed them."

Sean blew air hard over his lips and smiled. He shifted in the seat. She reached over and put her hand on his shoulder, grabbed the back of his neck firm. He closed his eyes a second and hung his head. Lifted it again.

"It's terrible what happened," she said.

He cleared his throat. She wouldn't stop trying to look him in the eye. He would only nod and sip at his beer.

HE GOT UP MID-MORNING AND started working on the condition of the room. About eleven the cart pulled up by the window and he heard a knock but told them to carry on. After a minute he went out and followed in the path of the cart until he found it. A young, ponytailed girl was inside one of the rooms turning down the bed, silver ring through her bottom lip. She turned to see him in the door and froze up a little. He had clean towels from the cart in his hands and asked if he could take them. She came over and took them out of his hands and swapped them out for proper-sized towels. She didn't say but a word. He went back to his room and kept at the cleaning.

Three hours later he walked through the service entrance at the hospice and travelled the corridors. He went to the opposite side of the building from where his old man had been living and started checking nameplates, door by door. He met a man shuffling past with a four-legged walker and that man waved and went on. O'Hara found the room he wanted right before a dogleg in the corridor. The door had been stoppered open and sunshine lit the hallway carpeting in a rhomboid shape. Sean went into the room and kicked the stopper clear.

DECARLO SLEPT IN HIS CHAIR near bolt straight. Nonetheless, his head lolled and he had a dried salt line aside the corner of his mouth. The man would have been perhaps six and a half feet tall were he to stand. O'Hara stood not quite six feet in work-boots, taller than his old man had ever been by an inch. DeCarlo had thick hair yet, white through and combed to the side. Elephantine ears with one lobe gone and the bottom cropped oddly. By the looks of it he still had most of his actual teeth.

Sean leaned in and shook him gentle by the shoulder. Like brickwork under the dress-flannels. When DeCarlo stirred he seemed to have trouble getting his lids up and then they just went all at once. O'Hara let go and sat back. Studied the big man's eyes. It was like looking into deep water.

"O'Hara?" the man said.

"Not the one you think."

"Are we playing cards tonight?"

"I told you, I ain't him. I'm his son."

DeCarlo sat forward slightly to better see.

"Where's he at?"

"You know where he is."

The old man fingered his cropped ear and hummed something. His hands shook considerable.

"You gonna tell me what happened between the two of you?" Sean said. "You miserable, evil bastard."

The old man frowned hard, shuffled in his seat. Sound of joints popping but it seemed not to bother him. For a few seconds they stared at each other and then the older man looked toward the window. Had to squint against the sun. Then at once he stood tall, patted his pants pockets and the breast-pocket of his shirt. Sat back down. In the sitting he reset himself. Looked like he might drift off again. Sean took his arm hard through the shirt. DeCarlo snapped to and tried to clear the arm. O'Hara held it fast with both hands and clamped it down to the chair.

"You killed him, know it? Knocked him down and knelt on his neck until he gave it up."

The man kept struggling to get his arm back. Sean had to stand.

"That wasn't yours to decide on you piece of shit. Ya hear me?"

DeCarlo just shook in the chair and started grunting, chuffing through his big teeth. He was looking all over the room when O'Hara cuffed him hard at the cheek with the flat of his hand. Short shot but loud in the room. The old man swatted the air where the hand had been and then grabbed his chairarms hard enough that one came loose. He stared at Sean and the younger man stood up. Something in there that had to be reckoned with. A minute by and no man moved. Then DeCarlo let go of the broken chairarm and started to fiddle with his ear again. His chest filled and sunk perhaps a half-foot by each hurried breath. Slowed and slowed. O'Hara sat back down in his chair and studied the man some more. They were like that when the orderly came into the room.

"You can't be in here," he said. "Who are you?"

"Payin' a visit."

"You family?"

"Not even a little."

"Do you know him?"

"I do."

O'Hara had already gotten up out of the chair when the orderly told him to leave. He saluted the orderly and went. He didn't look back to the old man.

IN THE TAVERN HE DRANK WHISKEY and beer and by midnight he'd piss-streaks down the leg of his jeans and no skin on the top two knuckles of his left hand. He sat at the bar turning a ragtowel red and when they tried to chuck him he pinned the back-bar mirror with an ashtray and leapt over and took a forty of Irish, swung it around like a cudgel. They'd no proper bouncers and he booted the door open himself while they were calling the cops. Someone called him a fucktard and he wheeled around to come back but the door was pulled shut and bolted and he hammered on it but a few times before he remembered how close the cop shop sat in relation to the tavern. O'Hara left the main street by a wooded pass and entered the lake gulley. Went knee-deep through dead leaves and damp brush. He carried the bottle yet but didn't open it. Truly he wasn't even that drunk. When he got to the hotel he saw to fixing that. Turned off all the room lights and left the TV flickering and drank from the whiskey bottle. He'd hooked a headset into his phone and listened to music in the dark. He sang crazily for a while. Then he started calling people.

HE WOKE UP IN RUINATION AND SHE was asleep sitting up in the bed beside him, shoulders against the headboard. She had a funny look on her face and snored tiny and she was as pretty as a woman would ever get for him however long he had left to know one. O'Hara had to piss with a fair bit of urgency but he wouldn't get up for fear of waking her. Odd light behind the windowshades either from the lot-lamps or the mustering of the sun but he couldn't tell which and shut his eyes awhile more. He did not sleep. She stirred just a few minutes later and laid her palms to either side of his head. He could feel her breath by his eyelid. She tugged his hair a little.

"You still asleep?" she said.

"Yep."

She let the hair go. Flatted it back with her fingers.

"Always you were bad at that," she said.

O'Hara put his hands to the mattress and slid himself back so that his neck crooked at the pillow and his elbow lay over her thigh. That was as far as he made it.

"You were in a state last night," she said.

"Anything good happen?" he said.

"Don't be stupid."

He tried to turn over but she held him fast. Put him back. She was under the covers and most of him was not but he got one arm past to where he could feel her dress-hem and the skin of her bare leg below. He put his forearm to the inside of her knee and his fingers about her ankle. Waited to see what would happen. She didn't clear him out but that was all. He lay there snookered.

"I thought you'd get married," she said.

"I did."

"Well, where is she now?"

"I don't know."

"What?"

"Northern California for a long while. Think she shuffled off to Oregon since. I've only heard what I've heard. An' that ain't much."

She ran through his hair again with both hands. Moved her forearm around the underside of his neck and her fingertips dug in at his left shoulder, thumb to his collarbone.

"You gonna be okay after I leave here?" she said.

"Yeah," he said.

"You sure?"

"Hell," he said. "I couldn't even buy my way into a scrap last night."

"That's not a big surprise."

"How's that?"

"It's a small town, Sean. They all know who your dad was."

He sat up in the bed and looked at her.

"You know what I mean."

"I'm the only one who really knows it."

O'Hara got clear of the bed and looked for his jeans. He found them and picked them up filthy and tossed them to the corner of the room. Went to the drawers. She sat at the edge of the motel bed and set about putting her shoes on.

"If you're just gonna go out lookin' for trouble again I can call the cop shop and tell 'em to make up a bunk for tonight."

"I ain't yours to worry about. Anyways, don't you know? You can get away with murder in this fucking town."

THERE WERE TWO SQUAD CARS OVER at the home when he passed by near dusk. Cops could be seen plain in the lot and he figured the rest to be inside with the old man DeCarlo. He cranked hard at the wheel and came around in the road, crested up into the frontlot. There he stomped the brake and slid short.

"Fuck it," he said.

O'Hara turned to see over his shoulder and backed out into the road again. He left at a good clip. In the rear-view he saw nothing and kept on. He'd been at the bottle again but only beer so far and he drove straight enough. No matter. As he reached the county line there were reds firing in his mirrors. He drove awhile and as calm as could be before he coasted over into the shoulder-sand and turned the key back. There were two cops that came to him and one was the older cop he'd seen the night his father had been throttled and the other was young and about as wide as he was tall. O'Hara wound the window open.

"Son, get out the damn car," said the older cop.

"Why?" said O'Hara.

The cop stood back a step with his thumbs hung in his belt. He stared. O'Hara opened the door and got out and sat on the hood of his own car. Crossed his arms. The cop eyeballed him hard and he didn't move an inch from where he stood.

"You didn't hurt him, right?" the cop said.

"Who?"

"Answer me like you know I'm not an idiot."

"I didn't. I just talked to him."

The cop eventually nodded. He spat in the road. Looked off to where no cars carried on the tarmac and looked back to the young cop who had already spelled off toward their cruiser.

"You know I went to school with your dad. Well, not directly. We were a few years apart. But we saw each other around."

"Okay."

"I wasn't his friend per se. But I did like the man. Once we ended up on the same side of an unwinnable kind of scrap and by God he won it. I don't even know how it started but I'll remember him in it long as I live."

Sean stared over blankly, bit his upper lip and nodded once. The cop nearly said something else but he stopped and then he unhitched his thumbs. Around them the daylight crept out and the last of it spread low on the fields and behind croprow lines of hand-planted firs.

"If you'll carry on thataways back to the city I'll just shake your hand and say so long. How 'bout that?"

O'Hara got off the hood. The old cop stayed exactly in place. His partner had started coming back over in a hurry and the older cop froze him with a glance. The old cop held out his gigantic hand and O'Hara took it firm and looked him in the eye. When they let go the cop paused a beat as if to take the boy's stock and then he walked back to his car. He didn't get in and he didn't get in. Finally Sean went around his own vehicle and settled into the seat. Lit up the ignition. He peeled out from the gravelsand enough that it kicked all over and then the tires caught asphalt and he continued southwest by that winding roadway.

BY TWILIGHT HE SAW THE TURNOFF posting and he kept going until the last he could, and there he hauled the wheel around and skipped over the macadam and the close corner of the turnoff curbing, churned turf there a second or two before getting out of the muck to the road proper. He pinned another beer and the incline helped him drain it.

The village streets were sparely lamplit and when O'Hara left the main road there were no lights at all save for those that burned behind housecurtains and dropped blinds. He coasted slow until he found the street again and there he drew up against the curb and shut off the engine, left the radio playing and the window open. He must have slept because when he shook awake the clock digits had climbed by hours. O'Hara looked to his left and right and to the right he could see a man bent down and watching him through the passenger-side window frame. He was about as big a man as you could get.

"You're parked out front the wrong house, bud," said the man.

O'Hara stared over at him and started smiling funny. The man shook his head and walked away over the front lawn and toward the lit porch of the small house. O'Hara squinted hard against the near-dark and saw the man's truck in the drive and a woman looking out from behind the outer screen door of the porch. Sheetmetal mailbox not three feet from the car with "DeCarlo" stencilled into it. He could see no toys nor bikes nor paddling pools. He called out and the man stopped in the yard and turned, mountainous and anvil-headed. O'Hara opened his door and got out. He set his feet in roadgravel and rose full, liked it enough.

Above him bats pinwheeled in the warm night air and carried past. He went around the car and started up the asphalt drive to where the man stood waiting.

HUNTED BY COYOTES

SQUEAK SAID HE COULD hear coyotes trailing us through the dark of the field. Heard them getting closer to us as we went.

"You ain't," I told him. "There's nothin' for 'em to eat off your skinny ass."

The kid had just come outta high school a year before, lived with his parents up in the north end of the city. We were working there, way up past A Hundred and Seventieth Avenue. New subdivisions all around and roads half-built, mud and gravel and silt. Like old carriage roads in frontier towns of the eighteen hundreds. Between those neighbourhoods were prairie fields of snarled and dying highgrass. You could smell snow in the air but it hadn't yet come in earnest. Any day. We walked in near blackness through a field from one neighbourhood to another. Highstepped over barbed-wire fences and helped each other through the lines. Squeak once got caught and in getting him free we all but tore the ass out of his pants. He dropped his work-binder and out came papers and pens and some of the papers were the deals he'd signed that day. One of them lifted up and floated off on the wind and I chased it down to the street and stomped it flat.

"Hey. You didn't get a code on this one," I said.

Squeak came up with a hitch in his step, trying to both walk and check out the hole in his workpants. He took the paper from me, smiled as he did.

"They didn't have time to confirm that shit on the call. I just got him to sign and told him they'd call later."

"You know you got about a twelve percent fuckin' chance of that bein' worth anything in the end?"

Squeak laughed.

We went on, door to door on either side of the road. Some people were home and some people weren't. In that city a late autumn evening came on early, streetlights on at four p.m. and the true dark of night by six-thirty. We worked until nine, or so we were told. Most houses were lights-off with people in bed or out of town for work. You never knew how many people actually lived in a neighbourhood yet. Me and Squeak went from one house to the next, got a few people to answer and stare at us through their screen doors like we had three heads. Some of them listened to us talk and try to sign them up and some of them pretty much told us to take a hike. We went for an hour with nothing to show for it and when I got to the end of the last drive in the row Squeak was waiting there for me.

"My side sucks," he said. "I'm goin' to the bar."

"Where?"

He pointed out across the nearby field at a far-off plaza and a set of new stores, signlights plain in the distance.

"You comin'?" he said.

I stared at the lights and made a fart sound over my lips.

"Fuck. I'll do one more street. Then I'll meet ya."

HE KEPT CALLING MY PHONE when I was inside the house with a well-to-do middle-aged couple. I ignored it and went on with the deal. They signed up and I phoned the call centre from the house line. Got the code. Gave the man his copy and shook his hand and told them to have a good night. When I came out onto the front porch Squeak was right there, pale as could be.

"I'm bein' hunted by coyotes," he said.

"What the hell are you sayin,' man?"

"They followed me 'cross the field again. I could hear those sons of bitches callin' out to each other. They're right by the fence on the other side of the street. They wouldn't stop comin'."

I walked down the drive and out into the road. Squeak tried to get hold of me by the tail of my work-shirt but he couldn't hold on. He hung back and I stood in the middle of the street, lamplight behind me from the houses and blackness in front. I started to laugh and heckle at Squeak over my shoulder when a set of yellow eyes lit up in the shadow. I got serious real quick. Then two more sets of eyes came to be and floated by through the murk.

"I told you they were out there," Squeak said. "I was waitin' for one to step out and then I was comin' right into that house with ya."

"Do we got the ability to make fire?" I said.

"I don't have anything."

I looked back at the house. Thought about how crazy they'd think we were if we holed up in there. I took the papers for my deal and stuffed them into the binder. That was money I could lose by giving those people doubt and I needed that money bad.

I started out of there on the part-finished sidewalk on the built side of the street. Squeak walked beside me on the front lawns to the houses.

"Stay in the light where I can see you, kid."

WE MET THE REST OF THE CREW up in Whitecourt. Drove there in Squeak's beater car. The heater ran in fits and starts and Squeak had to put his mitts and hat on. That fall had been long and mild but you could taste winter in the air, more so the farther north we travelled. When we got into town the rest of the crew was at a double-stacked motel with a lot full of rigs and jacked pickups. Most of them were already out at the cars holding photocopied maps with areas high-lighted on them by Ben, who had recently taken over running our crew. Me and him were friends enough before that, but now he had a job to do. I waited for him to assign an area of town for me and Squeak. As I was standing there I saw another buddy of mine, Matt, coming out from his second-floor room. Half-awake with his clothes on cock-eyed. He held the door open. Out walked one of the girls from our crew. She waited for Matt to lock up and said something at him as he passed by. Then she followed him down the steps and pretended not to see me standing there at all.

"Squeak," Ben said, and gave him a map. "You're workin' with Jessica today. You all can take her car. I got some good area for you guys."

Squeak looked back at me and I just shook my head. He went on. She'd gone clear around the lot and Squeak met her at her hatchback and got in. As soon as he got his feet in the car they were driving off.

"You're workin' with me today, buddy," Ben said. He wore a shiteating grin and backhanded me on the arm with his binder. He looked me in the eyes. "It'll be good. I scoped out a spot on the way into town. It's gold. Trust me."

"Where's fuckin' Matt workin' at today?" I said.

"He's out on his own. Some area he's worked up here before."

I just nodded.

BEN DROVE US ON AND ON PAST fresh-planted subdivisions. Godawful McMansions and modest new bungalows for young people starting out, big yards and wooden fencing and double-driveways. A few times we happened upon some older places of brick and hardwood, farmhouses that had stood up to an age of seasons bleak and brutal, buildings that waited solemn for the coming winter. We passed all of that by and drove over a forestbound railway crossing and there we travelled dirtroads and ended up in a rundown trailer park at the edge of town. Lousy units

with battered metal siding and broken screen doors.
Nicer double-wides with full gardens shrivelled to
the soilbed. Other trailers with front porches built
on and old men sitting out with tallboys of Pilsner in
the early afternoon.

"I fuckin' love TPs," Ben said.

I was going to tell him that there was something
wrong with his brain but I knew we were about to
pull over and go to work and my guts wouldn't let me
talk for all their turning.

We were circling the park on opposite sides of the
roadway. Ben skipping from door to door like he was
trick or treating. After every knock I had a few seconds where I prayed nobody was home, but I talked
to those poor folks that answered anyway. Tried to
explain to them the benefits of fixing in energy rates
for five years. I took noes no problem. Went on and
got the few easy sign-ups that I could, thankful just
to have some numbers. Ben didn't take any noes well.
He had long since figured out how to disassociate
and keep on with the pitch. He was the best agent in
the whole outfit.

Halfway through the park I had two deals. Ben
had nine. He was having trouble stuffing that last
one into the slip in his binder, fat as it was. Those
papers with his chickenscratch writing on them
would get him six hundred and thirty dollars, and
it wasn't yet dinnertime. We took a break and Ben
smoked.

"You aren't gonna go all crazy on Matt when we
get back, are ya?"

"She wasn't ever my girlfriend. It's a dirty fuckin'
move though."

"There's only so many girls on a crew. This shit happens."

"It's like fuckin' high school. Bunch of hyenas circling. Nobody follows any rules."

"Just stay positive, man," Ben told me. "We're gonna make a bunch of money on this trip. That's the whole point of everything."

About a half hour later I came to a trailer with sorry, busted toys all over the decking. There were no vehicles in the drive but the lights were on, and I could smell a fry-up from where I stood at the door. I knocked. When the door came open I could see nobody, but then I looked down and there was a small boy standing there. The kid was five or six years old with training underwear on. No pants and no shoes. Wrinkled T-shirt with a Polaris logo on the front. In his upturned hand he held a mittful of pan-fried perogies, grease dripping down his little forearm. He picked one off with the other hand and took a bite of it. The kid could have been dirtier. His face and his hair appeared to have been washed with water at the very least.

"Hey bud," I said. "Are your folks around?"

He shook his head.

"My mom's at work."

"You know when she'll be back?"

"Who're you?"

"I'm just here about the gas and power. No big deal."

He ate another perogy and studied me. I looked around the trailer and saw a living room with a couch and an old TV, a science fiction movie playing through the VCR. Some kids had made a spaceship out of a washing machine by the looks of it. There was a pile of clothes in one corner of the room and a pile of firewood in the other. The kitchen came right off the living room and he had the greasy frying pan on the lit burner of an ancient electric stove.

"Dude. How long has your mom been at work for?"

The kid looked up and mouthed a silent count.

"Three days."

"Jesus Murphy."

The kid looked out past me for a second. Dusk settling in heavy on the park. He started shuffling back behind the door.

"I better go," he said.

I started to say something but couldn't figure out what it was and then the door was shut. I stood there a long time and then I got off the porch and walked on down the lane.

Two men were yelling down from their deck at Ben when I got to him, cans of beer in their hands. They kept trying to wave him off and get him to leave but he just stood there with his binder, a goofy look on his face, his creased-up pants all but hanging off his ass. The men were in jeans and workjackets. Dirty ball cap on the one doing most of the yelling.

"I know what kind of scam you're runnin'. People in here got burned before on this. What d'you think you're tryin' to do?"

"Tryin' to save you some money. If you don't want to save money that's up to you," Ben said to him.

"Get outta here."

Ben turned around in a circle and looked up and down the gravel road.

"Get out?"

"Yeah. Get the fuck outta here."

"Get out of what? I'm not in anywhere."

The man pitched his half-empty beer can at Ben. Ben stepped to the side and watched it go by. He started to laugh and walk toward the porch all at once. I got over between him and the men up there.

"D'you know there's a little kid down the way who ain't seen his mom in days," I told them. "He's all on his own. You guys know where the mom's at?"

The men didn't seem to care for the story. One of them spat.

"She'll be back soon enough. She always comes back there sooner or later. Now go on."

"I should call social services and get 'em down here is what I think."

"You'd have to be an even bigger asshole than you already are to do that?"

"How's that?"

"You call it in and that boy'll end up in a foster home or a fuckin' orphanage until she gets him back, or until she doesn't. Didn't think about that though did ya, whiz kid?"

"You are special," Ben said to the guy. "Are you aware of exactly how special you are?"

The man stood up tall and went into the trailer. The other one started smiling. He took a pull from his beer and then made a pistol of the fingers on his free hand and dropped the hammer. Ben gestured like he was jerking off at the guy. But he did it while we were leaving, and we left that place pretty quick.

STORMCLOUDS HAD COME TO Grande Prairie in the night while we slept two to a bed in a motel filled with loggers from interior B.C. In the morning we walked through a foot of snow to get to the cars. We ate and went out to our areas. I'd been paired up with my old buddy Matt. Ben drove us out to work in his van with some of the others. Dropped us off two by two. Often that was the way. To not let people take their own cars unless you had to. Strand them somewhere so they had nothing to do but knock doors.

An hour after when we were supposed to start, me and Matt were sitting on a pair of industrial cable spools that had been left behind at the edge of the newly built subdivision. The snow came down relentless. Flakes as big as a quarter. I kept leaning down to pick up a handful of snow to eat. Matt just stared out into the white. You could hear a lonely train horn bellowing somewhere behind the firs that bordered that neighbourhood. Where those cars were going up there or with what I couldn't guess.

"So you aren't pissed off at me?" he said.

"Not really," I said. "More at her. Not that I'm happy about it."

"Well, me neither," he said. "She won't talk to me no more anyway."

"No?"

"Let's go to work," he said, and highstepped out toward the road.

I'D GONE NEAR SNOWBLIND BY THE END of the first street. I couldn't barely see the other side of the road and I couldn't see Matt anywhere. Somehow I'd signed up two people, both men in their early twenties, both on their days off between ten-day hauls on the rigs. The oldest was younger than me by five years, but he owned a new house and had a pregnant young wife sitting bowlegged on the couch. All smiles the both of them. I felt a rumbling in my pocket and took off a glove and got out my phone. It was Matt texting me.

At the end of the road. It said.

When I got there he was back on the wooden spool. His binder lay four inches down in the snowpack.

"I'm goin' back to the hotel. Try this shit again tomorrow," he said to me.

I sat down on that other spool.

"You can come with me or not. But I'm goin'."

"Just come down and work a street. It's good in there. Get a couple deals and then we'll both fuck off."

He shook his head. Wouldn't even look back at the houses.

"Already called the cab," he said.

"You sure?" I said.

"I can't do it," he said. "Fuck it."

"Come on, man."

"I believe I'll blow my fuckin' brains out if I have to knock another door today."

TWO OF THE NEW GUYS WEREN'T AT breakfast the next morning. When Ben went up to their room they were long gone and the maid was cleaning. Matt left out alone to work in a nearby town. Me and Squeak were paired up again and Ben drove us out to our area, Jessica in the passenger seat of his van and she wouldn't say more than a word to me. They dropped us off and went to work together.

We were suited up for minus-ten weather, and for more snow, but the skies had cleared to pale blue and the sun shone down at us. Squeak went door to door and I half-worked the other side of the street but more or less just cherrypicked newer houses. By three in the afternoon Squeak was all piss and vinegar, smiling ear to ear. I picked him off with a snowball when he came out of the last house. He flailed and went down into the powder on their front lawn. Lay there laughing his ass off. He'd already signed up five people. That was the most he'd ever done in a whole day.

We stopped at a redneck bar and ate a late lunch. They had a grizzly bear's head mounted over the centre of the backbar. Four roughnecks were sitting at a booth-table in the back and one of them was passed out, slumped over against the corner of his bench-seat and the rude brick wall beside the booth. He sounded like a lawnmower. By the time we got out of there it was maybe four-thirty and the sun had dropped behind firs and foothills to the west.

Two hours later we were working in the dark of night. Splitting up blocks of fourplexes and townhouses. Squeak couldn't get another deal. I signed four people up and by eight o'clock we'd nearly spent the whole area. I let Squeak work the last set of townies. Found a beat up playground in the middle of the townhouse block and sat on the merry-go-round. Spun myself around by little sidesteps. Squeak did not come out for a long fucking time. I tried to text him but he didn't text back. I called and he wouldn't pick up. I watched a jackrabbit edge out from the shadow and half-stand, nose twitching. I stood up slow. He froze. I came off the go-round at a full sprint and the rabbit bolted, leapt the low-end of a teeter-totter and bounded away four feet at a time. I walked back to gather up my binder, hauling cold air as fast as my lungs could take it in.

When I got to the door of the last townie Squeak was already coming out. There was a very good-looking thirty-something-year-old woman in a night-gown and she was letting him out. She had tired, pretty eyes, the careful movements of a studied drunk. Squeak pulled the door shut behind him and nearly ran right into me. His hair stood up all over the place and his shirt was on backwards under his coat. He'd lost his snow pants somehow.

"You gotta be kiddin' me," I said.

Squeak started to grin like an idiot. He walked down off the step and we made our way across the housing block. The kid looked like he had just been told the meaning of life.

"Did you just take that broad down?"

"It was pretty much the other way around."

"So you're tellin' me you just got your v-card took in there?"

Squeak just shook his head.

"I didn't have a rubber."

"My God."

"And she owned a fourplex across the way. I signed them all up for her."

"What?"

"Then I believe she smoked a bunch of meth. Out of a glass pipe. Naked as the day she was born."

I stuck my binder out to hold him up.

"How d'you know that?"

"They were rocks that she put in it. Fuckin' meth rocks."

"Jesus. Wait. You didn't smoke none of that shit, did ya?"

"Fuck no. I was terrified."

We got out of that neighbourhood and called Ben. Told him to come get us by that hillbilly bar. I went in and bought twelve bottles of beer on off-sales and we drank at it outside while we waited.

"How d'you feel?" I said. "Now that you're supposed to be a man and all."

"This is the single weirdest day of my life," Squeak said.

BY OUR NEXT ROAD TRIP WE'D LOST half the crew. Matt had taken to working alone most days and he barely did that. Jessica had been planning to make enough money to go to California, but instead she'd lost her shit and moved back to Saskatoon. Even Ben was trying to figure out a way to give it up and move back east but he had debts up to his eyeballs and he was scared to quit. Squeak didn't sign one single deal in the week after we got back from Grande Prairie. Ben couldn't get him on the phone. One morning Squeak's binder and his badge were just sitting there on the secretary's desk in the main office. That was the last anyone heard from the kid.

I'd gained thirty pounds since starting that job and was drinking beer every night after work. I would drink until three in the morning and then be up and out to the office by eleven. I never did a full day's work anymore. I worked alone most of the time. Ben set up the next road trip to Lethbridge because nobody was signing any deals in the city. He said everyone had to go or they'd be fired. Two more people handed in their badges before we drove south.

A chinook blew through that town the whole time we were there. It got as high as eighteen degrees outside but the wind ripped hard and if you weren't in a jacket by evening you were very cold. Ben tried to make me work with other people but we pulled shit numbers so he made me work alone, stranded me way out at the edge of town or in half-built subdivisions with man-made ponds and vistas of highgrass dunes and far-off bluffs broken by narrow rivers and waterways that were barely more than sand-slurries. At one house I had a beer with a young girl who went to college in town. She had blonde hair and a piercing in her nose and bottom lip, tattoos on her slender arms. She told me she was from a little town in B.C. and we talked about places we came from. She was very nice to me. By the second beer her boyfriend came through the front door. I thought there might be trouble but he shook my hand and sat down beside her and had a beer as well. They were good people. I took a beer for the road and walked very long and lonely through the streets.

I worked blocks of townhouses and pulled more than a few deals. A bunch of the people I signed up were Plains Indians of the Blood tribe. At least that's what I was told. I had papers with names on them like: Melissa Eagletallfeathers. Joseph Broadhead. Sally Longtimesquirrel. At the end of one block an enormous man opened the door for me. He went about six-foot-six and two hundred and eighty pounds. Long hair and dark, dark eyes. We sat in his living room and I signed him up. He told me he was an actor and he'd been shooting a big movie down in Mexico. I knew of it even though it wasn't all shot yet. He said he was away all the time and needed to keep the bills in check for his young wife. He showed me a picture of her and their baby. When I left his house he shook my hand and thanked me and I left that neighbourhood and walked far out of my area. Hours until I saw another new development at the town limits. I cut through barren, windblown fields and aimed for the densest set of houses.

The sun had long since started to set and now shone red at the horizon. No trees or buildings or bluffs to shield it. I stared down to the southern plains and might have been seeing clear to Montana, flat as that stretch of territory was. I couldn't keep my eyes open long for all the sand and grit that flew on those ruthless gusts. In the end I dropped my jacket and unbuttoned my shirt. Put the jacket back on over my undershirt. Tied my workshirt around my head like a Bedouin headscarf. I walked like that until I heard a far-off whoop. Then a high-pitched chuckling that carried. I looked back in the half-light and saw small rounds bobbing on the distant plain. They got bigger after a minute.

By the time I came to the rude boundary fence for the subdivision I had wicked shinsplints from hustling over the hard ground. I went through a gap in the fence and looked over my shoulder. The coyotes were maybe fifty feet behind me. Three of them. I came back to the fence and kicked at the rough timber until a couple of narrow pickets popped their nails and broke loose. I picked them up and went on down a gravel trail between half-built houses. Stray Typar wrap trailed out from one house and rattled hard on the chinook wind. I went across the fresh-laid asphalt of the subdivision circle road and beelined toward a gazebo that sat over a central man-made pond, wooden bridges coming out to it from the four corners of the neighbourhood. There was only pale light left to the west and there were no streetlamps on that side of the place. My shoes touched bridgeplank and I started to run.

As I climbed up the side-latticing on the gazebo I could hear the drumbeat of paws on the bridge behind me. I cursed out my fattened guts as I hauled myself up and over to the top of the thing, rolled over huffing and stared up at the prairie sky, vast and star-speckled. I shimmied up to the peak of the gazebo roof with the two pickets in my hand. There I sat and watched the coyotes saunter close and stop. All stared up with their slanted eyes and outsized ears, narrow snouts. Thick-tailed dogs with coarse fur the colour of straw. The alpha whooped.

"Fuck off you ugly mutt," I yelled at him.

I took a handful of roadgravel out of my pocket and starting pitching the heavier stones at them. They spooked and skittered back. Then they all loped onto the gazebo platform, spread out and circled the thing. Whenever I got a clean look at one of them I pelted it with gravelrock. I nailed a squat-looking dog right between the eyes and it bucked and yelped, started to growl. I lay back on the roof and heaved air, felt the round of my stomach through my workjacket. A hard square of metal up near my chest, under the jacketcloth.

"Yes," I said.

I lay there drinking whiskey from the flask and listened to the coyotes padding around on the platform, jostling against each other. The wind whistled in my ears. I had gotten very warm from fighting with the coyotes and from the drink. I took my jacket off and it had but cleared my hand when the wind tore it loose and threw it down to the coyotes. I sat up quick and got to my haunches at the edge of the rooftop. The coat had been flung down atop the squat coyote and the animal was tangled up in it somehow, snout stuck in the armsleeve by the look of it. He pinwheeled hard and banged off the wooden railing at the edge of the platform. As he spun I saw my badge fly from the coat and drop into the pondwater below. Then I saw my phone skittering out across the decking. It stopped face-down, one weak shove away from going over into the water. I drank deep from the flask and put it in my back pocket, took up the stakes I'd pulled earlier and leapt down near right on top of the trapped coyote. The other two had come over to check out the commotion and they scattered when I landed. I beat hell from the dog under the coat and he snarled and cried and then ran away crazily, bounced off the sidefencing all the way down the near length of bridge. One coyote had fled and circled around the gazebo. He came back now and took up behind the alpha. I pitched a stake at the alpha and it went end over end and hit him hard in the side. He hollered and the other coyote fled halfway down the bridge and stopped. I ran at them screaming bloody murder. The alpha ran and so did the other. Down they went to the road and the pass we'd come through and then they were trailing the coat-covered coyote as he scrambled blindly over the plain. Blue cloth and blue jacket sleeves flapping hard and then all three dogs lost to the dark.

I went over and picked my phone up from the deck. Called Ben and let it ring long until he picked up.

"What is it?" he said.

"Come out here and get me. I'm way the fuck off the map."

"It's only eight o'clock."

"I could give a fuck what time it is. You're comin'. Now hold on a sec while I figure out where the fuck I'm at."

A MONTH LATER WE WERE AT THE opposite end of the province. All the way up in Fort McMurray. Bitter cold. Fields and forests thick with snow. We were on the third week of a three-week trip. Ben had lost nearly all of the crew and there were only five of us up there. Matt had come on the road but he hadn't worked more than a few days on the whole trip. We'd taken on another guy, Charles, who had worked for the company before and quit to sell dope for his cousin, a low-rung Vietnamese gangster. The cousin had got himself pinched a few weeks before and Charles was back knocking doors.

They put me with Charles for the third week and we worked terraces on the west end of town. One day there was a thaw and the cold broke. Sun

on the runnels of meltwater trailing down drive-
ways and sidewalks. The next night the temperature dropped thirty degrees and froze the roads to
sheer ice. The sun stayed out but shone down grim
where eight-foot icicles hung from roof ledges.
Trucks spun out and went sideways down neighbourhood streets. Charles had dressed badly for the
trip and he was griping the whole time. I gave him
my toque and gloves to keep him quiet. We were
sliding all over on the way to the front doors of the
townies, houses with stained wood panelling and
tall firs in the yards.

"I'm gonna wipe out and I fuckin' know it," he
said.

"Just don't fuckin' panic when you hit a patch.
And slow down."

"I'm freezin' my balls right off. I gotta keep
movin'."

I got into a house across the road with a middle-aged fellow from Newfoundland, took a beer
from the man and sat with him at his kitchen table.
He told me he'd come west to the prairies ten years
back and wanted to go home nine years and eleven
months ago. But the money was too good. He had
two kids born and raised up in McMurray but his
wife was an east-coaster, just as homesick as he was.
He told me he didn't know if he should sign up and I
told him not to worry about it. I drank the beer and
sat a few minutes more and then I went out. I felt bad
to have even knocked on his door.

When I got back across the road Charles was
talking to a chubby kid that looked about thirteen.
Jacked pickup in the drive with forty-inch roughtread

tires, windows tinted black. Charles asked the kid if his parents were home.

"This is my place, bud," he said.

"Really? How old are you, dude?"

"Turn seventeen in a week."

"Jesus Christ," Charles said.

The kid signed up with Charles and went back inside. Charles came down the drive shaking his head. He slipped once and skittered around the walkway. Got his feet back under him.

"You hear that shit?" he said.

"Yep."

We walked down the sloping neighbourhood road, Charles counting his deals. I didn't have to. I had four and that was enough to coast on. Charles had six. A busted tavern sat about a hundred yards away, across the bordering street and beyond a frostbitten field. Ravens alit on the bar's roof and some strutted the snow atop the fieldgrass. Pecked hard through the icepack. They were nearly two feet from beakpoint to tailfeather.

"What time is it?" Charles said.

I just smiled.

"You think we could get four hours outta that bar?"

"I think so, Chuck."

"Don't call me that. Let's go."

Charles had skateboard shoes with worthless treads and he went slow down the grade. He grabbed at my coat arm. I was a good eighty pounds heavier than he and I righted him. Held him up. He let go and went on. Not two steps later he lost it and he was in the air, arms all over.

"FUCKIN' WHORES."

His binder flew maybe fifteen feet and hit the deck long after he was flat on the ice and sliding starfished down the hill. I got to his binders as the papers were slipping out the side. I stuffed them back into the plastic sleeves and took the binder up, skated down the hill backwards with my shoetoes and palms against the ice. At the bottom I helped Charles back up and batted the snow and grit off his ass and back with his binder. Handed the thing back to him. We got over to the side of the road and he stood there cursing the universe. As we found our bearings the monstertruck rolled down slow over the grade and skidded short to a stop at the end of the road. The sixteen-year-old kid was at the wheel. He waved at us and then gunned the engine, fishtailed out into the cross street and drove on.

THE NEXT DAY WE WERE OUT AT THE northern edge of town, knocking doors of a subdivision that was half prefab houses and half luxury trailers. All riggers, pipeline workers, transients with nonsensical hours of work. Off in the distance there were gasfires burning from the skyward exhaust pipes of a gargantuan refinery. Black plumes of smoke gone heavenward. Pale blue high above and a yellow sun that arced but three-quarters of the way up into the sky before starting back down. Charles had bought real winter boots now and had a goosedown coat over layers and layers. He had outfitted himself entire with ski-gloves, a toque, sunglasses, and an aerated facemask.

"What are you, fuckin' ski-ninja?" I said.

"Well, I don't got all the beer insulation you do, you goddamn walrus. And I can't grow a fuckin' beard to save my life. Too Asian for this shit."

We took sides of the road and knocked for a few hours. Either nobody was home or we were waking them up. Charles signed one young wife and while he was inside I went on knocking. I got to the end of the road soon enough and looked back for Charles. He had stopped for a smoke and I saw him going up the driveway of a new house in a set of three, all of them unfinished with plastic on the windows and huge coverflaps of carpet fastened to hang down over the doorless garages. Charles went through the flap and held it back so I could see a propane torpedo heater firing in the middle of the laid concrete, like a miniature jet engine that they ran to let fresh-laid concrete cure and to keep the foundations from cracking in the bitter cold. He gave me the finger and let the flap down. I went to the last house in my row.

When the door opened I was looking at a young guy in a wheelchair. About my age. He had a cup-holder fixed to the right arm of his chair. Tallboy in the holder. He wore a hoodie and cargo pants, a huge brace and bracket over the whole of his left pantleg. That foot was up on a stirrup fixed to the chair and the other one was shoed and flat on the carpet. He was tall and broad-shouldered and looked like he'd probably been a pretty athletic guy at some point.

"Well, come in and shut the door, bud," he said. "It's near goddamn forty below out there."

I did go in. Followed him through the small house. Clutter of old pizza boxes, beer cans, piles of clothes on the floor and none seemed dirty. He had a huge flatscreen and he'd been playing video games on it. He told me to grab a seat and I sat down on the end of his couch. The young man wheeled into the kitchen and disappeared behind the partition there. I saw his hand go up to the fridge door and pull the handle. Rattling. The sharp thud of things being knocked over to the glass shelving inside. The door shut and the man came back with two tallboys.

"Will you have a brew?"

"Probably I shouldn't. I gotta work awhile more today."

"I don't trust a man who won't take a drink."

"Me neither," I said. He smiled and pitched the can over. I caught it.

I gave him the spiel and he stopped me partway. Beckoned with his fingers for the forms.

"My wife always turns you guys down," he said. "But anything to save some dough sounds good to me."

"She gonna give you shit for signin' up? I don't want to get you in any trouble, man."

He shook his head. Kept filling out the forms.

"She's at her sister's awhile. Out in Golden."

He gave me back the forms and I called it in. The young man went back into the kitchen and could be heard bashing around in there. I looked at the pictures on the living room mantle. The man in his hockey gear with a team. The man with his blonde wife, dimpled cheeks, very young. The man in his coveralls, welding mask in his hand, standing high up on the crossbeams of a massive rigtower. Before I got the confirmation code from the call centre I pressed the talk button with my thumb and the phone went dead. I kept talking.

Wrote nonsense on the forms. The man rolled back into the living room with another two cans.

"You're all set," I said.

"Sweet."

"If you don't mind me askin,' man, what's the story on the leg? How long you laid up with it?"

"It ain't the leg," he said, and knocked on the knee joint of the bracing. "Well, it is, but that ain't the problem."

"How d'you mean?"

"My back's broke."

I just stared at him. Nodded slow. Tried to be cool.

"Ain't nothin' to be done," he said. "But the fuckin' company's tryin' to stop me gettin' paid for it. Didn't have the right insurance they say. That's why things are tight 'round here."

"They'll pay up soon enough," I said.

He frowned. Took a big pull from the can. Wiped his mouth with the back of his hand. I drank the can he gave me in gulps. Shook his hand and said so long.

WHEN I CAME OUT OF THE HOUSE I SAW Charles way up the street. He was fiddling with the latch of a metal fencegate in the front yard of a new red and white double-wide. Then I saw him leap the locked gate, hustle up the porchstairs and knock at the door. Cold air froze my nostril snot as I walked up to the road. My eyeballs felt funny. I left my gloves off long enough to pull out the last contract I signed and ball it up in my hand. I stuck the crumpled deal in my pocket and put the gloves on. When I looked up again Charles wasn't at the door and he wasn't in the yard.

I heard him before I saw him. Cussing and growling. The sound of held breath that came out all at once. I passed his binder, splayed face-down in the road, and went on. There he rollicked on the sidewalk near to the fencegate, clutching at his ass and upper hamstring. There were streaks of red in the white where he'd gone and now blood pooled small in the packed-down snow underneath him and started to freeze there.

"What'd you do?"

"Fuckin' slipped trying to jump the fence. Fuck."

"Who d'you think you are? Jackie Joyner-Kersee?"

"I will fucking kill everyone."

I turned him over and he tried to fight me off. Reeled off all the colourful language he knew through gritted teeth.

"Let me look at it, you dummy," I said.

There was a lot less blood than I thought there'd be but still more that you'd ever want coming out of a hole in your asscheek. There were crystallized gobs of frozen red on his torn-up pants and upper leg. Furrow dug deep into the meat, welling slow.

"You'll get a bunch of fuckin' stitches but otherwise you ain't got that much to worry about," I said. "I'll get on the horn with Ben. Just keep pressure on that goddamned thing."

Charles scooped a handful of clean snow with his glove and pressed it onto the wound. He lay there on the ground with his face in the crook of his arm, shaking his head, breathing hard. I stood and waited for Ben to pick up, studied the aluminum teeth that gabled the fencetop. A long strip of black pantcloth from the kid's outers trailed from one point, tendril of pale skin pasted near bloodless to the lining.

THEY TOOK CHARLES TO THE HOSPITAL and left me out there in the late afternoon dusk. I had five hours of work left is what I was told. I sat down on a piece of plywood in a new buildsite, watched the sky go to black around the refineries to the north. Labyrinthine pipework. Those exhaust pillars with their gasfire tongues. Brighter now against the black. I was very fucking cold. Everything in the world was evil. All the dogs were trying to kill us. I got up.

In I went through the carpetflap that covered the garage. The torpedo heater roared. I sat on the warm patch of cured concrete beside it and sniffed hard at the fumes. I played games on my phone until I was afraid it would die and Ben wouldn't know where to get me. I pulled out the flask and set it on the ground to let the chill metal warm up. When it did I drank at the whiskey. The garage covers did not move at all. Not one gust of wind. Sound of a critter passing in the snowpack outside. Raven cries somewhere in the night. I drank on and shaped shadows on the raw-timber wall.

ON THE LAST NIGHT OF THE TRIP I worked alone in a trailer park beside the highway, right before you come into the town proper. They dropped me off in the area late and as soon as they were gone I walked through half-frozen bogland to get to a nearby gas station, ate a hot dog and bought a bunch of junk food. I shot the shit with the attendant for a while and then headed back to the TP. There had been another thaw and I read a temperature of minus four on a filthy thermometer that hung on the bashed-in metal siding of the first trailer I knocked.

Nobody answered that door and nobody answered the next one. I wove through the trailer park rows for hours. Boots thick with mud and shit. The neighbourhood had been set up in those highwayside lowlands with just one dirt road exit. There were stray cats wandering the place, barncat look to them. One house had a sailboat in the backyard on wooden railtie risers, no topmast. I went around some kid's Big Wheel that had been left in the middle of the street, came to a trailhead between two far-apart lots and walked out into the woods behind the houses. Forest of tall, lean firs. I pissed in the snow and tried to write the word "fuck." On the walk back I knelt down and picked up a handful of spent buckshot casings, studied the shells and tossed them clear. I went back to the park and started knocking another row.

After nightfall I could see lights in the windows of some trailers, could guess who was home and who wasn't. Nobody would answer the doors though and I didn't knock more than once. In near utter blackness I climbed the steps to the last trailer in a long row, saw lamplight inside through shitty drapes that looked to be made of bathtowels. A beater pickup sat crooked in the drive. I knocked.

The man opened the door with no shirt on, not a pinch of fat on him. Wiry arms. Knuckles big and busted. Shaggy brown hair gone grey around the ears. He had some fancy script tattooed on his left shoulder. I went through the routine and he watched me blankly, cold blue eyes studying my jacket, the binder, my hands. He smiled. All the right teeth were there but I could tell that the top set were ceramics. He waved me in and after a second I went. There were empty cans of Red Bull all over his living room table, old coffee cups. Brokedown couch with rough blankets over top of it. The trailer had a scent to it but it wasn't too bad. All in all, other than the clutter on the table and the patchwork furniture, the place was pretty clean.

The man went to the kitchen and came back with two coffee mugs. He held the one out to me and I took it and saw the black brew inside. Drank at it. The man sat on the edge of his couch with his elbows resting on his knees. He took reading glasses up from somewhere between the empties and put them on. Read the papers close. He held his hand out and I gave him a pen. He signed and handed the papers over. Settled back on the couch.

"That's an unusual job, what you got," he said.

"You're tellin' me."

"You come up from the city?"

"Yeah," I said. "We go all over the place. Try to get up here as much as we can."

The man raised his eyebrows.

"You from here?" I said.

"Son, nobody's from here."

He'd emptied the mug and said he was going for a refill, pointed at my cup. I waved him off. He went to the kitchen.

"You got any beers in there?"

"No," he said. "I don't keep 'em on hand no more."

He came back again and looked me up and down.

"Hang on," he said. "I'll get you a place to rest your weary bones."

The man went over to a chair aside his couch. He reached behind it and got hold of something. I'd seen the metal poking up from over the top of the chairback but it hadn't registered at the time. When he stood up straight he had the barrel of a moose-rifle in his hand and he carried the rifle over to where he'd been sitting and leaned it up against the arm of the couch. He held his hand out toward the chair.

I sat in the chair and drank the coffee slow.

"When you gotta work 'til?" he said.

"Nine."

"That's an awful late hour in the middle of winter."

I nodded. Settled back in the chair. I had the binder resting on top of my right leg. I looked at it awhile. The man wouldn't quit staring. I finished the coffee and set the empty mug down on the table.

"You must see a lot of weird shit, goin' into peoples' houses of a night."

"All the time," I said.

He nodded.

"Well…" I said, and slapped my hands on my knees. Stood up.

He shuffled in his seat and got up to meet me. We shook hands. The man sat back down.

"Be careful out there," he said.

"Will do."

"You never know what folks are gonna be like, they see you walkin' around in the dark out there. Somebody's liable to shoot ya."

It went quiet for a time. Then he started to laugh and I laughed with him. I didn't force it or fake it even a little. I laughed full out as I put my boots on and I was still at it when I turned the doorknob and stepped out under dim porchlight. I waved at the man as I shut the door and he waved back. Down I went by his rickety shortstairs and soon enough I was walking the dark rows again, collar turned up against the nightwind.

SHAPE OF A SITTING MAN

WHEN ARTHUR LEAPT OUT from the black the eight men around the fire quit talking. One stood like he was pulled up by cables. The fire burned six feet high in the quarry-pit gulley and showed the skin of Arthur's legs painted with dirt and ran through where he'd been cut by rock and thorn on the way down the grade. He passed through those seated on stumps and stooped near the fire to take up a long and knotted cedar limb, black by the thick end. He stepped outside of the circle of men and turned. Little lights yet travelled the wood when he clubbed the nearest man across the brow bone with it. That man half-rose with a hand by his face, soot black forehead torn and swelling.

"That's from Bill Cooper, you motherfucker," Arthur said.

The next shot loosed smoldering charwood from the branch and sent the man sidelong into the bonfire. Arthur ran hell-bent at the grade and climbed fast while the men below hollered and tried to pull their friend clear.

HE CAME TO THE TRAILHEAD and broke left through the pines. Footfalls on the hard ground nearby. He ran into the Merritt girl blind and they both went down into the bracken. He'd just got his bearings and started to stand when she laid into him about the neck and face. Rings on her right hand split him on the cheek. He got her wrists and wrestled her back, tripped her, sat on her legs. She bucked her hips but couldn't get him off.

"Jesus," he said. "Quit fuckin' fightin' me."

"What'd you do?" she said.

She settled a little and Arthur stood, let her up. She whacked him again and he just took it.

"This is why you were hangin' around me for? Ain't it?" said Merritt.

"Let's just get in the car."

"I'm not drivin' you anywheres. You son of a bitch."

They stood there looking at each other. Arthur tall and wide by the shoulders, dark eyes and dark hair. The blonde Merritt girl with a horse-bite scar through part of her chin. Out from the pit came battle cries. Boots on the hillside. Nucleuses of fire carried up on logs and sticks. Arthur grabbed the girl's head in both hands and kissed her by the temple.

"I ain't sorry," he said, and took off down the trail. Partway down he realized he had but one shoe on. He kicked through a sapling with his shod foot and kept going.

THE TRAIL SHOWED IN FLASHES OF shallow moonlight. He had thumped a pint of whiskey on the ride out there and it didn't hit him until he was deep, deep into the wood. He puked airplane fuel into a patch of ferns. Arthur did not know the trail by sight, but it sloped down toward the northeast and to town. So down he went. He had been terrified that they would have dogs but he heard none.

By the time his feet found tarmac the stockinged foot was cut and bloodied. To his left the narrow concession lanes ran long and vanished into the black. The half-moon and pinhole stars were dimmed by passing cloud and Arthur could see little that told him where he was. He turned right and loped away, his gait getting stranger and stranger by the damaged foot. Finally he had to stop and he got down to his knees and put his head in his hands, hauled air too deep and choked on it. He got up and went on. A few minutes more and he saw incandescents burning high behind the treeline. A crossroad there with fresh-laid asphalt and a metal gate. Steelwork shape of a boat welded to the barrier.

INSIDE THE MARINA GROUNDS ARTHUR moved in shadow and went wide around the boathouse. He came to a length of pier and hobbled to the end. Little lights aglow in the distance. Brightest from the town's silica refinery and bayside grain elevators. Arthur looked down to the waters and he could hear but couldn't see them. He leaned in like he might dive and then his legs felt funny and he went sideways, landed forearm down on the cement pier-top.

"Fucker," he said.

He got to his feet and went back, started along a drawn-out line of boat slips, most of them empty, the dock-lengths bobbing but slightly in the water. He found a twenty-five footer with its covers on and he waited on his haunches. Not a sound. He climbed up onto the stern by a short ladder. The pegs and button-ties of the vinyl coverings were thick with dust and grit. Arthur popped enough of them to slide under, face first to the aft deck and the cabin door.

Arthur couldn't get the door open. The locks were inside the door itself and he had nothing to pry with or break the thing down. He lay there on the decking and held his shoulders. Fifteen minutes passed and his teeth were clacking. The shoeless foot hurt from the cold. He sat up and stuck his head out through the unfastened coverflap. After a minute he climbed back out and went low past the docks again.

THE DOOR OF THE OLD TRAWLER was made of wood and pinned shut with a rusted padlock. Arthur lay on his back with his hands braced against a battered deck-box. He kicked with both feet and the door blew inward, swung back at him and rested crooked in the jamb. He crawled inside and found benchseats laid over with canvas seat cushions. Arthur stripped them and dropped one length of padding on the bare cabin floor, lay under the others and turtled. He fairly shook but couldn't see his breath. He reached down and took the sodden wool sock off his one foot, rubbed at the thing with both hands. It ached and sang by the nerves.

HE WOKE UP WITH HIS EYELIDS wound all the way back. The boat listed slightly and settled again. Shuffling on the aft deck, outside the broken door. Arthur squatted there in the cushions and waited. He could see movement by the broken framing. He scrambled around the cabin and came back with an expired fire extinguisher for a weapon. When the door opened, he squeezed the trigger and let fly a tepid cloud of white. No more in the cylinder. He raised it like a cudgel and nearly swung but didn't.

The Merritt girl dropped something heavy in the doorway. She had white powder in her hair and on the skin of her face.

"Jesus fucking Christ," Arthur said.

"What the fuck is wrong with you?" she said. "I can't see a goddamn thing."

Arthur shoved by and took her hand and went out onto the deck. He eyeballed the row of boat slips and the grounds and the hills beyond. Nothing moving that he could make out. By the rear seat he found an old bait can stained light with dried soil. He reached over the bow and dunked the can in baywater. Shook it and tipped it and dipped again. This time he got hold of Merritt and poured the water on her face. She hollered and tried to spin away. Arthur put his hand over her mouth and she opened her eyes wide. She hit him behind the ear with her palmheel. Arthur sat down on the deck and the can rattled clear and fell to the black waters. Merritt wiped at her eyes with her shirtsleeve. Arthur looked around again and went back inside the cabin. She had dropped a whiskey bottle and he found it and took a huge pull. She came back inside.

"How'd you trail me?" he said.

"You son of a bitch," she said.

"Quiet down, will ya."

She cussed him out until he crowded her and put his hand back over her mouth. She bowled him over to the cushions and he just held her there by his left forearm. Muffled threats and calls for murder in his right palm. Her hand went inside his belt where he was hard as could be. She gripped him fierce and worked, her elbow running a furrow on his front from belly to sternum. He took his hand away and tried to kiss her too sudden. Teeth clacked on teeth. They had their tongues flicking at each other's and he got her jeans unbuttoned and off over her hips in one downward tug, underwear and all. She made a funny sound as the cold hit her ass. Arthur had his buckle sprung and pulled his own jeans off, cleared but one foot from the cuff before she climbed on.

WITH THE BOTTLE MOSTLY GONE they dozed, back in their clothes, too cold was the night air through the broken door. Arthur's guts took a spin or two and settled. Merritt's head lay warm on his chest and she snored small. He studied her for a long time.

HE WOKE ALONE IN PALE LIGHT. Grey shades of dawn and the eerie sound of loon cries. Swamp life humming and chuckling from without. He was chilled to the bone, his shirtback damp with cooled sweat. Arthur cast about the cabin for signs of the girl. Nothing but the empty bottle and her better smell. He edged the door open and saw the sun huge and barely risen over the marsh. Dewbeads on the decking and not a tread or footprint left there. She had left him some time ago.

Arthur searched the boat, drunk yet but sharp enough. In a cupboard he found two distress flares layered with dust. The first a rocket-flare to fire by hand and the other a beacon-flare to plant. He laid them by. He pulled a cushion-cover loose and set about folding it into some kind of bootie for his bare foot. He tore bits of fabric into strips to tie it on. He walked the deck unevenly and then stepped up to the stern and opened his fly. The skin of his dick hurt bad as he pulled back against the cold to piss. The last staccato lines of urine killed him to shove past, and still he felt like he hadn't loosed all there was. Arthur zipped and was about to get down when he heard voices carrying from somewhere behind the treeline. They came again and louder by far. His heart thumped even though it was broke in the places that counted.

"What've you done to me?" he said.

Arthur fired the rocket-flare from the deck and watched it sail. Then he lit the beacon-flare and left it burning on top of the cabin. He wiped his shoe-sole on cushion fabric and then eased down onto the dock, walked carefully and left little in the way of prints. On the lot-concrete he took off and ran hard to the west, coasting the shoreline where the marsh ran shallow. He heard a diesel engine rumbling low from somewhere in the marina lanes. Men calling his name over and over, bellows from the cousin of the man that Arthur had laid down face first in the bonfire coals that many hours ago. If there was a female voice in the pack he couldn't tell. He went down the bank and into the soup.

Arthur's legs were numb throughout before he'd slogged ten yards across the swampway pass. His balls had gone and his hurt-dick didn't complain anymore. The bogwater reached high on his chest at the deepest, cattails and lily pads sliding past and catching his shirtcloth. Gnats and mosquitoes spun clouds above the putrid catchwater pooling stagnant in the hollows of pinned tree branches. He went as fast as he could without drawing attention to himself, without risking a misstep in a pocket of riverbed mush and going under entirely. The men were on the boat now. The beacon-flare went spiralling against the blue, blue morning sky and landed out in the bay. Arthur Cooper travelled on.

A hundred yards out in the marsh he found the other bank. He had young, bowed willows to help his cover as he eased up the rise on all fours. When he cleared the water he looked back. On the other bank he saw the Merritt girl standing with one hand to shield her eyes. She dropped the hand and stared a second more. Moved along. He shuffled off through the swampwoods.

THE TV WAS PLAYING LOUD ON THE back porch of the little house when Arthur came through the yard at a stagger. It was mid-morning and the sun had scorched his shoulders and the backs of his ears. Huge pines shaded the crabgrassed yard and most of the house. Great shape of a sitting man through the porch screen. Arthur announced himself in a rasp and then went heavy up the wooden steps.

Bill Cooper watched the TV from his armchair, slippered feet tapping on a throw rug like they were working piano pedals. When Arthur came in the man turned slow. Eyes ringed underneath and his unwashed hair sticking out from the side of his head. He lifted one massive, knobbled hand off the chairarm and put it back. Smoke circled up from the other hand and hung thin below the ceiling. Ashtray nearby full of butts. Bill Cooper's left eyelid would not open all the way. A thick cranial scar started just below his hairline and mostly hid under his thick, black hair.

"Late gettin' home," Bill said.

Arthur nodded. Touched his brother on the shoulder. He went through to the kitchen and took a beer from the fridge. He twisted the cap loose and drank it down in two pulls. Stood the empty on the counter and got another and went back to the porch. A folding chair stood near the wall and he set it up.

"You sit out here all night?" Arthur said.

"Couldn't sleep."

Arthur slumped on the busted chair and sipped. Bill stared at Arthur long and then started turning back to the TV. He moved like he was underwater always, messages part-delivered by his nerves. Stew of medications in the blood. For all of that his feet and legs would not quit their little dance on the chair and on the floor. The big man reached up to smoke in short, repetitious drags, his fingernails bitten through to the quick.

They sat together and didn't talk anymore. After a while Arthur watched Bill's head start to nod and then loll to the left against the chair back. Arthur got the lit smoke from between Bill's fingers and stubbed it out. Waved at the air. Then he went through the house and locked all the doors and windows. Pulled the drapes and the porch-shutters. He took the coverings from his bed and laid them over his brother. Shut off the television. Arthur sat there wretched in the dark, his ruined foot in a basin of hot water and antiseptic. The big man whispered things in his sleep. Arthur listened and listened.

DEBRIS

COME PALE MORNING THE OLD woman found a greycoat squirrel drifting dead in the swimming pool waters. It travelled slow to the south end, trawling leaves and surface algae. Pegged there its wasted tail stropped the lip-molding. Emily Moore stood outside the short-fence with her roughskinned palms resting atop the arrowhead pickets. Beyond the pool and the little farmhouse were acres of untended field. Wildgrass and rogue wheats the colour of desert sand. A tractor half-sunk into black, black soil. Two silos ringed with rusted boltwork, old lettering worn faint and unreadable.

"Bob," she said loud. "We got another in the pool."

Nobody answered so she turned and made for the sliding doors to the kitchen, open yet with the drawn curtains rolling against the wind. He came out before she got there.

"Yes dear. You called."

"Oh shh," she said. "Get that net and your shovel."

The old man stood a head taller than her, broad-shouldered and bowlegged, heavy plaids and worn-out jeans.

"How big a hole we gonna need? My back ain't my best friend today."

"Ah," she said. Looked over to the pool. "Maybe three scoops. No more'n four. The poor little fella saw less winters than he should have."

THEY INTERRED THE SQUIRREL IN THE DAMP, dark soil. Tucked him in with the flat of the shovelhead and pinned a tree branch cross there at the head of his small plot. That potter's ground had dozens more crosses set in awkward rows, very few lost to wear and weather. Emily had written on all of them in black ink, such things as: "Raccoon. Spring. 1998." Markers had likewise been posted for chipmunks, groundhogs, rabbits, one wayward cat. The old man had complained early on about the burials but it turned out that if they didn't lay out the bodies his wife couldn't sleep at night. So he'd quit his griping and kept at the planting. No prayers were said.

EMILY WALKED THE GROUNDS maybe a mile out from the house, following the length of a long and bending stream. There were blockages where water built and ran humped over sodden leaves. The old woman carried a cherry-branch walking stick and she worked the little dams loose and watched the current take them on bit by bit. An hour past and she could see rainclouds and their vaporous tailings. Steadily they went with the rains below like shuffling fibres. Her knees were singing to her about the humidity. She'd had to retie her long, grey hair more than once on the walk and now she just let it blow about the shoulders of her overcoat.

"Jeez, it's close," she said.

On the way back the day turned eerie and very dim. A sparrow flock boomed from a huge and naked oak out in the fields, wound themselves inside out and took off to the north. Emily left the creekline and headed across the fields toward the farmhouse. She had very good eyes and she could see Bob out in the backlot, like a toy figure stood there. He raised one hand and pointed at the skies that shifted behind her. Emily didn't look.

WINDS WHIPPED THE LITTLE house while they lay in their places in bed. They'd left the window slit-open and it whistled at them. The drapes were near sideways for minutes at a time. Emily's bedside lamp had its bulb turned low and she had laid her book down beside it a long time ago to study the sounds of that storm. Thunderclaps landed like atomics and could be felt by the bedsprings. She had thought the weathers would carry past but it all seemed to have sat down and settled right in that farmstead. Finally she reached up into the lamp and turned the key. The room didn't go truly dark somehow. Once in a while fork-lightning flashed white daylight through the curtaincloth, scented the air with electric.

"This is a bad one, ain't it?" Bob said.

"Yes. I don't remember the last like it."

He had corralled her in against him and she let him. His arms with their cord-muscle and mean elbow knobs, skin soft as old paper. She closed her eyes and then opened them again.

"Jesus H. Christ," she said. "What the hell is that?"

"I took one a' them pills," he said.

"When?"

"Few hours ago."

Emily whacked him on the thigh through the covers. The two of them lay there quiet for a while with the rains battering the roofshingles.

"Well..." she said, and turned around, took his face in her hands.

THE KITCHEN ENTRANCEWAY FAIRLY shone near sunrise. Emily had the door open and the floor tiles were warming under her bare feet. The storm had picked up debris from across the county and seemed to have flung the all of it down on their plot. Emily waited for Bob to dress while she brewed coffee on the stove. She thought the power would be out for sure but it wasn't or at least wasn't anymore.

They went outside in their coveralls and boots and Bob made for the garage and his barrow and work tools. A length of eavestrough had come loose at one end of the building and he had to shift it wide to get the door open. Emily watched him fuss with the thing for a few seconds and then she walked out from the house. She'd not made it to the poolside fencing and yet she knew something was wrong in there. The waters were dark with steeped mud, and thatchwork layers of leaves and sticks lay over entire sections of the pool. Near the centre a young woman's white body carried past in a torn nightgown, lower back and ass up at the surface while her arms and legs and hair dangled like she was reaching for something at the bottom.

Emily didn't know how she got over the fence but she was over and bone-sore in her legs. She called back toward the house. Her hand searched the water for part of the girl's gown but it couldn't reach. When she got into the pool the cold all but stopped her heart.

THE BODY LAY UNDER A SHEET ON the stonework behind the house for the better part of the morning. The police had come by the dozen and they'd studied the pool and the girl and they'd surveyed the farmgrounds that sucked the boots right off their feet. A towering, ginger-haired cop called McGuire spoke to Emily and Bob at their kitchen table, his hat over his knee joint. He asked them a few questions and none too hard. Emily sat swaddled in so many blankets that she could barely stand when the cop got up and put his hat back on. McGuire smiled and she shook his huge hand before the cop left out to get his instructions from the newly landed detectives.

By evening they were very much alone. Bob had gone back outside and tried to work against the creeping dark, stacking the loose breakwood into a teepee as tall as he was, great mound of leaves and long grass underneath. While he worked by twilight Emily ran a bath, sat there on the closed-over toilet watching the tub fill up. She had a bottle of beer in her hand and there were two empties on the bathroom countertop beside her. She drank the last of the one she had and took the bottles out to the kitchen. Came back with another beer and again sat there waiting. When the tubwater started gurgling down the overflow she went over and turned the taps. Emily started to take her robe off and then stopped. She stared down into the tub for a minute. Then she reached in and yanked the plug.

When she came back outside Bob had already lit the stack. It smoldered low at the heart, the pilings too dense and too damp yet. Emily shut the sliding door and walked over to him with two beers in hand, offered him the one. Bob looked her up and down.

"You okay?" he said.

"Okay as I'll get today," she said.

He put his left arm around her like they were gone to the drive-in. Smoke started railing out from somewhere in the build and carried up into the dusk. Flash of yellow. Nothing. Leaves started curling.

"Here 'tis," she said.

OVER THE MOTTLED FIELDS SHE went. Half an hour out she got to the treeline and scoped the firs. The sun hung high and furious but the inner woods were lit only in patches. Emily walked on over the forest floor and its pine-needle carpeting.

She had the cherry-stick and used it to shift face-height branches, cobwebs thick as string that broke and trailed ghostly from their peggings. Eventually she reached a break in the trees, a shieldrock ridge that looked out over a low clearing. A narrow clay path led down to the place in a series of switch-backs. Emily didn't go any farther.

A cabin sat crooked on the grounds below, no more than three rooms. Satellite outhouse with a shovel-dug shithole. The place had foundered a little on the southwest end but the windows and doors were intact and the frames square. Nothing stirred. Still, Emily waited there for the better part of an hour before she started down the grade.

SHE MADE IT BACK TO THEIR FIELDS in time to see her husband on the drive back from town. His truck rolled tiny in the distance, spitting dust on the concession road before it turned off for their long lane-way. Bob parked and went into the house and came out again, looked around. Went back inside.

He was in the john when she came through and hung up her coat. She waited for him in the kitchen but she didn't sit, just leaned her hip to the sink-counter. He pissed loud and quieter and louder yet, sound plain as could be with the door wide open. Little one-shots afterward that rung the bowl. Out he came cinching his belt on the walk. When he saw her standing there he stopped for a second and coughed. Kept on with the buckle before stuffing in his shirt-tails.

"You know nobody can sneak up on me," he said.

She blew air hard over her lips.

Bob went over to the counter, brushed his shoulder against hers as he passed. He started up the stove-burner and left the coffee pot to brew atop it.

"Did you go by the cop shop?" she said.

"I did."

"They find her people."

"There ain't any people."

Emily shook her head.

"I don't think I can believe that. Even if it is true."

Bob nodded. He set a cup down for her and then poured another. When he sat at the table he didn't drink and he didn't talk.

"What else?" Emily said.

"They said the girl had a blood-alcohol level that coulda sat a buffalo down. As well as her veins were run through with Benzodiazepine."

Emily put her hand to her mouth for a minute and let it drop. She stared out the windowglass at the muckfields. Bob turned in his chair.

"Tell me you ain't been out there through the woods," he said.

Emily sipped at her coffee.

"He's covered his tracks pretty well," she said. "But that little son of a bitch is livin' in that shack."

"Come on now."

"I just don't know for how long he's been there," she said.

TWO MORNINGS LATER EMILY found the backdoor to the garage swinging on the breeze. Little marks by the keyhole cylinder. She had Bob inventory his tools and whatever valuables he could think of. In the end he had lost only a Phillips screwdriver and a half-gallon of Varsol. He said he would've been happier were the truck gone.

They fished a blue jay out of the pool the next morning and couldn't figure out how he got in there and how he couldn't fly off when he did. They'd slept little and Bob dragged ass when he went for his burial tools. He came back with a wood-handled trowel, the blade tarnished by the edges.

"Where's your shovel?" Emily said.

"I do not know."

She just looked at him, shoebox in her hands that carried the little birdbody.

When they made it to the plots they stood bewildered for maybe five minutes before Emily dropped the box and headed back to the house. Bob called after her but she couldn't be turned. He knelt awkward on the turf, bit at his bottom lip as he found a workable position. Then he dug the hole with the trowel and tipped the shoebox. Beyond him in the makeshift graveyard all the crosses had been plucked and they were gone and the naked soils told no stories anymore about who they'd put under. The old man tamped earth down in the new plot and kept eyeballing the grounds to see what else might be out there with him.

A LONE CRUISER SAT IN THE road in front of the farmhouse. Officer McGuire heard Emily out as he stood on the flagstones behind the kitchen door and then he walked the fields, got smaller and smaller until the trees took him. An hour later he resurfaced at another opening perhaps a hundred yards to the west and made his way back to the house. He had red lines in his cheeks and forehead from the branches he'd caught. His boots had doubled in size by the mud and he left them outside and stood beside the kitchen counter in his stockinged feet.

"If anyone's staying out there I couldn't tell," he said.

"He is," Emily said. "You could see it's been disturbed."

"I did everythin' but bust into the place," said McGuire. "Sure, there's signs that it's been tampered with. But that could be raccoons or kids or god-damned anything."

"It's the son," she said.

The cop looked to Bob and he just clamped his lips together and shook his head but once.

"The last anyone saw him he was banged up in Moosejaw and then supposedly put in hospital out west. Even then they were petty charges," said the cop.

"It's known pretty well that he did things he didn't catch a charge for," she said. "Even a young man like you has to have heard it."

"I've heard a lot of things," the cop said. "And I know the elder Campbell was a murderous son of a bitch but there just isn't anything to say that it carried in the genes."

Emily got up from the table and took the cop's huge forearm in both hands through his jacket. Looked long into his eyes.

"I hope that's the truth. 'Cause I was in school with the father."

McGuire stared back at her for a few moments and then down at the counter. Cleared his throat.

"You got my card to call me," the cop said. "I'm not kiddin' when I say you can get me on the horn anytime if something's up."

"Okay," she said.

McGuire took his hat up off the counter and put it on. He stood high enough that his elbow sent a rack of hung pans rattling. He stopped them one by one. Then he went out with a nod and set about bashing his mud-caked boots together in the yard.

TWO WEEKS LATER ANOTHER GIRL was found half-eaten by a fertilizer slurry pit, this on a soy farm not ten miles away from Emily and Bob's place. The cops came out to collect her body. The girl had been lost after a bush party, left out walking down the county road with her friend, both of them sixteen years old. The friend still hadn't turned up. This time there were news trucks at the site and special investigators down from the city. There were floodlights ablaze on those grounds until after midnight and the farmer who lived there was kept under watch until the cops cleared him of any part in it and went back to guesswork and conjecture.

The next morning two squad cars pulled up outside while Emily was frying eggs. Four cops came to the door and they were all bruisers, but none as big as McGuire. He stood front and centre when Emily opened up for them.

"There any way to get to that shack in a vehicle?" he asked her.

"Not with what you've got," she said. "But you can drive out across the rocky part a' those fields if you want. Save you all but the trail-hike."

McGuire tipped his hat to her and all of the cops went back to their cruisers. They rolled up over the curb and carried on through the highgrass, bucked hard as they made for the treeline.

THAT EVENING AFTER DINNER BOB lay slumped in his armchair with his belt unbuckled and his thumbs hooked into the strapleather. Emily shook him by the shoulder. He stared at her wide-eyed. He was the kind that woke up all at once and she'd always been impressed by it.

"What is it, Em?" he said.

"I think I'd like to go to mass."

She wore a red blouse and a long skirt that swam about her ankles. Her hair was pulled back tight to a ponytail.

"Well, alright," Bob said, and set about putting his pants on proper.

THEY'D GONE TO THE OLD CHURCH on the hill. It had a lookout tower at the height of the grounds that saw over the entire county, the big inland river and the sea that it came from. Emily lit a five-dollar candle before mass. Candles set in three rows of glass tubes with the most of them aflame. The rows went upward to a plateau where the bones of Jesuit priests were kept in cases of wood and gold. Finger bones of the one. Part of a pelvis. Sheared-off shortribs. An entire skull sat on a narrow cushion in the largest encasement, a rectangular hole punched into it above one aural canal. Upon the darkwood walls of the church were pegs full with old crutches, canes, bracings. After the mass they were quick to get out of their pew, but Emily stopped and came back to the candles and lit three more and then she went out. She'd not paid for any of those and Bob didn't bring it up.

THERE WERE LEAVES AND BAUBLES of knotted wildgrass in the entryway when they got home, the front door open and drifting. Bob started to go inside and Emily grabbed a fistful of his shirtcloth.

"You don't go in like that," she said.

"What?"

"Are you kidding me, Bob?"

The old man stared into the dim-lit house and he was breathing very hard. He shook his head and stepped out. Took hold of Emily at the elbow and moved her ahead of him. Walked back to the truck. There he asked Emily to get inside but she would only wait on the liner-step while he called the police. She tried to see into the almost pure dark on the property flanks. She could not see a damn thing. Bob got off the phone and they both climbed into the truck and locked the doors and then Bob backed out quick and drove to the concession fork where they would see the cops clear on the approach.

Waiting there they watched him come out into the road in a hunch, stepping nimbly between over the middle line of a barbed-wire fence, perhaps fifty yards from where they idled. He stood tall and full and looked all around. Emily nearly ducked but froze halfway. The Campbell boy had a short, dark beard and a good head of hair and decent clothes. He wore a backpack and seemed to be cinching it tighter. He loped across the road and in five strides he was gone. Bob started to put the truck in gear.

"My God," Emily said. "Do we run him over?"

That caused Bob to switch his foot back to the brake and hold the truck. After a long, long minute the driver-side mirror lit in colours. Bob shifted into park again and waited with his one leg dancing on the floormatting. Emily reached over and steadied it by the kneecap. She spoke to him softly until they were not in the road alone anymore.

THE POLICE COULD NOT LOCATE Campbell and over the months to come they searched the cabin and the grounds so many times they were forced to move on. Sightings were called in from highway rest stops, diners, officers in other small towns as far as ten hours' drive away. No new bodies turned up that could be attributed to the killer, and those he'd already made were buried in the town cemetery according to which side of the fence a Lutheran, or Presbyterian, or Catholic Jesus lived on. Emily and Bob paid out of pocket so that a small stone stood for the first girl, who nobody had come to collect or shed a tear over. When the snows came that stone became awful hard to find.

Toward Christmas Bob took ill and had fever dreams and delirium that scared Emily. In the early days of it the only symptom of sickness he had was that he kept feeling like he had to crap even when he'd just emptied his bowels. They'd not thought much of it until he was cold always, weak by his legs. Soon he had two lumps form in his asscrack just below the tailbone and in three days it got to where he couldn't walk or sit and Emily drove him to the emergency room in the town hospital. He'd been taking her leftover hysterectomy pills behind slugs of whiskey but still he had to lay sideways on the benchseat with his head in her lap.

"This is stupid," he said to her.

"I don't think so," she said.

The tires bucked on the snowpack and busted roadways and when they did Bob snarled and knuckled the flooring.

"Can't you drive any smoother?" he said.

"I can stomp the brake and see if that don't put you to sleep until we get there."

"Sweet Jesus," he said. "Come on now."

He got in to triage and gave his information standing, went through to an examination room at a hobble and lay face-down on the bed, his jeans pulled clear for his ass to show. There he shooed Emily but she wouldn't leave him.

"I've seen parts of you that you ain't ever gonna see," she said. "What more is there?"

"I don't like you seein' me sick like this."

"It's fine."

"Hell it is," he said. The words were part-muffled by the pillow. He kept his face there until the doctor came in. The doc knew the name of Bob's malady within seconds and it would have been called boils when they were younger but medicine called it a cyst now. It bothered Emily to hear it. She stood and squeezed Bob's hand and he just looked at her. Then she did leave.

SHE GATHERED HIM CLEAN underwear and folded it neatly on the bed. Made up a small bag with his toothbrush in it along with other necessaries. She came out to the kitchen and looked at the clock. Went for the cupboard and pulled a bottle of the good whiskey and poured a small glass. The little house interior showed strange in the haphazard lighting that she'd made by flicking whatever switches caught her eye on the way through. The kitchen was almost entirely dark and Emily was dark inside it when the Campbell boy passed by the sliding doors and could be seen plain through the vertical blinds by the glow of the full and low-hanging moon. Emily stopped where she stood and so did her drink and so did her heart. She waited a minute after he'd gone before she went to the bedroom and dug under their bed for the rifle.

He was quarterway across the field toward the woods when she stepped out onto the cold concrete and sighted him in the lunar pale. The killer Campbell made his way slowly with the snow high on his shins. Emily had no coat on and his shape started to shake against the sight. She cussed herself out and went back into the house and came back with a toque pulled over her ears and with her coat unfastened and drifting on a gentle easterly. Nobody was out there anymore. Emily looked and looked and then she pulled off her hat and pitched it into the snow.

WHEN HER HUSBAND WAS DISCHARGED home Emily tried to tend to him as he lay sideways watching nature shows on the television. He wore just boxer shorts and a T-shirt and his legs were patchy with grey hair but otherwise had muscle that seemed younger than the rest of him by decades. He'd often get up and shuffle over to the bathroom or to the kitchen for another beer. Bob had been run through with saline and antibiotics and had colour in his face again and part of his appetite back. Every few hours he had to settle in a sitz bath of warm water and salt to keep the lanced skin of his asscrack from any chance of re-infection. Emily never had to bother him once to do it. He'd have the plastic basin rinsed and filled and sat over the toilet and rinsed afterward before she could tell him anything. He kept the clock by it and Emily knew that he must have been in a great deal of pain in the days before if he were so hell-bent on making sure he didn't forget them.

IN THE SMALL HOURS BEFORE DAWN Emily left the house and walked the fields. She had no flashlight but she saw the tracks clearly and trod in them to her knee. Every step felt unnatural to her and she thought about branching off through the snowpack but she did not want snow in her boots to wet her socks. She carried a leather shoulder bag and had the rifle slung high so that the butt wouldn't drub the white. The new sun was but a sliver when she broke the treeline and travelled on through the pine-row corridor.

She'd enough layers to last the day through and had to loose one to stop herself from sweating as she sat on a stump above the clearing. The sun could not reach the cabin yet and the building sat there in its crooked way, dark and weird and without life. When sunlight finally hit the hollow Emily backed off into thicker cover and shook pins and needles out of her feet. She took up a handful of snow and ate it in bites. It was then that she heard a dry pop, what she thought might be a tree limb that broke loose somewhere in the wood behind her. But the sound had not come from there. She got down low and edged out toward the shortcliff.

There she watched as a patch of ground behind the shack rose, only visible by the fir needles in the snow and by two perpendicular black lines that widened as the cellar hatch was lifted in fits by a man likely moving up a set of steps. Emily lay down on her front slowly. She had the rifle in both hands and readied and she drew the stock to her armpit. She dragged the shoulder bag in front of her as a rest. Her heart thumped and she tried to slow it. The hatch rose enough that she could see Campbell's face and the length of his arms raising the trapdoor. She pulled. Crack of riflefire in the hollow. The door fell shut again.

*

BOB HAULED A BARROWFUL OF PAVING stones and cement-mix from the truck to the garage. When he wheeled his way back he came upon a cruiser idling at the roadside. He eased the barrow down. The cop McGuire sat in the driver seat with no partner. The sidepanels were thick with claymud dried hard by the warm spring sun. The tires were filthy with runoff from the farmhouse lawn.

"Mornin'," Bob said.

"You all doin' okay out here?" McGuire said.

Bob nodded.

"We are," he said. "How're things with you?"

"Quiet," McGuire said. He raised his huge hand and put the car into gear and drove off down the county road.

In the house Emily slept late. She'd woken just once in the night and had hustled to the bathroom blind and by the memory of her footsoles and then came back to bed. Her dreams were many and each started strange on the heels of the one before. She dreamt of waters and blackwoods and a barn foundering and collapsing on itself while a lone dog scattered not fast enough in the sidefields. She dreamt of driving in a car with no roofcovers. She dreamt of the dead girls, daughters all and none of them hers.

Emily got up and brushed her teeth and combed through her hair for a little while. She stepped outside onto the sun-warmed pavestones behind the house. An early spring had brought the snows down to sopmush over the fields beyond. She wore her bathrobe and walked the cement in her slippers. Bob had drawn the poolcovers back and the waters were hung through with grit and grass and twigs. Emily took hold of the fencerail and studied the pool. She was about to go but stopped. There in the far shallows spun a tiny, brown body, held under by a tangle of mossy branchlets, the tail trailing wide and drawing in the water gently. After a long time watching it she went for the net.

MOST OF THE HOUSES HAD LOST THEIR LIGHTS

K AYLA GOT TO THE TAVERN near midnight and her husband was already shirtless and inconsolable. He'd put one man through a table and the other into the wall plaster. Matthew had gotten to highground and held it by standing atop a wooden riser with chairparts in either hand. Kayla pushed through a crowd to the emptied sitting room. There were still full plates and pint glasses on the tabletops. Nobody would go near him anymore.

He had a steak knife buried to the hilt in the meat of his shoulder and it bled a crimson streak down his front.

"Who stuck him with that knife?" Kayla said to the bartender.

"He did."

"What?"

"That fella in the wall raised a knife at him and he picked up another and stuck himself first."

"Good God," she said.

They had called the police as well but they'd called Kayla first, so many years had Matthew come to that watering hole. Kayla figured she had but minutes. She went over to him and waited there. He looked around like he might find an escape route. He stood about six-foot-two when he was on the ground proper and he had big shoulders and was well-muscled all the way through. With his build and his beard and the blood it looked like he could eat her alive. Kayla just reached up for him. Stared into his eyes.

"You gotta come back home," he said.

"How 'bout you get down off the table first."

She had him by the wrist when the cops came in through the saloon door. Kayla pulled him down and took the chair pieces out of his hands. She got him sitting on a bench with his back to the wall and stood where the cops couldn't get to him without rounding her.

"He's sick," she said. "And he's hurt. Don't make it worse."

There were three cops and they were all big or bigger. They studied the ruins of the place with their thumbs hung in their belts. The least huge cop had a hand by his pistol. He was told to go and see to the man in the wall. The other two looked blankly at each other and at Kayla and at the man bleeding all over the upholstery behind her. The ranking cop took off his hat and rubbed at his scalp with his palmheel.

A PSYCHIATRIC NURSE STATIONED with the near police precinct met Kayla outside the emergency room. Kayla had to commit him to the mental health centre involuntarily and could barely sign the forms for all that her hand shook. The cops had told her plain that he would go to prison if she didn't put him in.

"How long you all been married?" the nurse said.

"Two years," Kayla said.

"How long has he been sick?"

"He was sick when I married him."

THE ER DOCTORS HAD SEDATED HIM and drawn the knife out and tended to the wound. Matthew's forearms and ankles were tethered to the bed where he lay post-operation. Cops guarded him there and they guarded his transport across the city to the asylum. Kayla rode to the compound in the back of a police cruiser, her knees banging against the fore seats. She tried to talk to the nurse and the cop in the front but they could none of them hear each other very well.

At intake Kayla had more forms to fill out and a harried-looking shrink to talk to. The doctor seemed to have woke up minutes before, her blonde hair barely tied and her eyes crowfooted at the corners. She was otherwise quite pretty, perhaps ten years older than Kayla. They went down to the cafeteria and sat lonely with the thrum of vending machines and overhead vents cycling the air.

"Did you notice any change in him lately, leading up to this?" said the doctor.

"Yes," Kayla said.

"He stop taking his meds?"

"I believe he was rationing them when I left."

"You left him?"

"Probably I shouldn't have."

The doctor sipped at her coffee and made a face at it. She sipped again. She'd not brought anything to write with. Kayla thought that strange.

"He lost his job and went off the rails. I went to a motel for the night and just kind of stayed on."

"He didn't hurt you? Anything like that?"

Kayla just stared at the woman until she asked another question.

NEAR FOUR IN THE MORNING she got to see him through the glass of his room door and he slept shallow and his legs danced a little against the mattress. That was the last thing she saw before she left. The cops gave her a ride home and when Kayla got out they were studying the house and the numbers pinned to the brick. She followed the flagstone walk and went down a set of busted stairs to their little basement apartment. At first she couldn't find her keys. No matter. She turned the knob and shoved. The door hadn't been locked and she didn't know for how long it had been like that.

THREE DAYS BACK AT THE HOUSE and she had cleaned the place top to bottom. Picked up all of his clothes and laundered them, folded them neat and laid them neat in the drawers. She went to the store for groceries and came back with a pizza and a case of beer. On the walk home black clouds carried in the southern skies and the afternoon turned to night in a hurry.

By six in the evening the rains had overrun the city lowlands and babbled out through the sewer grates. The river swelled and lit out from its banks and sunk highway feeder roads. People swam on the parkway where a train had left the rails and turned over, floated on and on. Most of the houses had lost their lights and candles lined high windowsills where people watched the rains. There were no birds anywhere. Near midnight the moon shone massive behind lessening cloud.

The apartment was on the west end of the city under a tall and narrow Victorian house, built near a crest on a street that didn't go under. Through the storm Kayla stood in the basement stairwell drinking at her beer, kept going around the place to make sure there were no leaks or wet patches in the drywall. The house did not lose power. She watched movies until the small hours of morning and slept on a mattress and box spring set right on the flooring of their windowless bedroom.

WHEN KAYLA GOT UP THE NEXT DAY she found a shallow pool of cold water in the back room of the apartment, leakage already dried to silt along the outer wall of their living room. She started to clean at it with a mop and some ragged old towels. After that she planted fans around the room and pointed them to where the water had come in.

"It don't look that bad," she said.

She was about to call him out of the room and she stopped partway and felt strange. Hollows inside her.

She went through to the kitchen entry. Saw where Matthew always had to duck low under the covered underhang where the vents ran. Tiny spots of red in the spackling where he'd often caught his forehead travelling past. The landing steps outside were bone dry when she went there to lay out the rugs, the concrete near-white in the sun.

DAYS TO COME AND SHE NOTICED the smell. Like damp soil. Fieldrot or the mulch of a forest floor. She pulled the furniture away from the walls and saw the creeping-vine paintings of mold on the wood and along the floorboards. Kayla bleached it all to where she had to leave the house and sit out front for a while with the doors and windows open. The fans blew at the baseboards and drywall for days at a time. The lower half of the back-room wall started to sag and buckle.

Their landlord came through with his friend. Both of them small and black-haired. They broke into the wall and studied the rot and the foundation where it was run through with cracks and fissures. They spoke at each other in Mandarin and the friend, who was supposed to be the contractor, raised his voice and held bits of the wall in a gloved hand. He chucked the ruined stuff and left the place in a hurry, wouldn't come back into the room. The landlord said he would be back and then he left too. A few minutes later Kayla went out and stood at the front walk, looked around the neighbourhood. Across the road was a small crew of labourers. Two men who'd taken too much sun and their crew boss with the crest for a local plumber's union on his shirt. Kayla went across the road to them.

"You all thirsty? I got some cold beer."

They just looked at each other.

"You gotta come down to get 'em," she said, and left out across the street again. Their crew boss locked the work van by remote and followed but ten feet behind her.

Kayla gave them each a bottle and had them come through to the back. They stood there filthy and studied the room, sipped at their beers.

"They're gonna have to seal this up," said one labourer.

"Shit," the crew boss said. "They're gonna have to gut the whole fuckin' place. Dig down around the outer walls and fix the foundation."

"Can we still live here?" Kayla said.

"Not for long."

AN OLD MAN WITH NAVY TATTOOS ran the front counter of the rooming house and he studied Kayla's forms behind Plexiglas. Weird folk travelled the lobby. Two women howling drunk in the middle of the day. A young man missing his right arm at the elbow. The rates were not as low as they should have been. The clerk was supposed to call for references but he just scribbled something and gave her a key.

"That your truck out front?" he said, nodding out through the greased and cobwebbed glass doors.

"It is," Kayla said. "You think it's okay out there?"

"You got belongings inside?"

"Yeah."

"Then, no, it ain't."

He leaned down under the counter and came back with a pass card in a cellophane sleeve. He slid it to her by the shallow gulley under the glass.

"There's a little lot they reserve for the bossman and contractors that come through. You can park there for now. It's covered over."

"Thank you," Kayla said. She took the pass and stood there with the old man a minute. He tried to smile at her.

"How long you plannin' on stayin'?" he said, and he said it funny.

MATTHEW WOULDN'T SEE HER through his first month at the hospital. She went anyway and spoke to the shrink and to orderlies that knew him. They'd switched many of his old medications and taken him off some of them outright. In some cases he'd been getting doped so heavy with them that his blood and organs were full with toxins and the shrink figured he'd just about crossed into territory where he might have spent his liver.

"They likely weren't working properly for him when he was taking them like he was supposed to," the shrink said. "Even before he started his tinkering."

"That why he hit the bottle harder all of a sudden?" said Kayla.

"Could well be."

They'd sat down in the cafeteria again, the place half-full this time with staff and patients and their visitors. Sunlight through the ten-foot glass and in the pale floor tiles. The shrink had a plate of fries and she'd near cleaned it. Kayla did not eat.

"Can we make sure he don't have to see his old doctor again?"

"Yes. I'll just have to get you to sign something. He'll send his records. Are you planning on speaking to him?"

"More likely I'll go over there and shoot him," Kayla said.

The shrink laughed a little. Kayla didn't. The doctor ate her last three fries. She got up with the tray and Kayla followed her back to the offices to fill out the forms.

KAYLA DROPPED SOME BOOKS and clean clothes at the hospital. She waited long to learn the same thing. Learn it by the orderly shaking his head as he came back to his station. Kayla thanked him for nothing and then she went back to the rooming house. She walked into the lobby through one huge, swinging door and then went right back out through the other.

THE BARTENDER GAVE HER TWO drinks for every one she ordered. She felt like hugging him. By and by she got drunk and sat there watching the TV above the backbar. She played pinball in the pool-room and the board was fucked and she beat it to tilt more than once. Leaning at the bar top for another round she heard two men talking and lingered on.

"I'm tellin' ya he was a crazy sumbitch. Some sorta nervous breakdown or somethin'. There was nobody could talk reason to him."

"I thought you were buddies."

The first man blew hard over his lips. Drank deep.

"Only in that we spent too many hours in this same row a' barstools."

"Well…"

"Well nothin'. I always did find that fella fuckin' spun and he's probably best to be locked up. He weren't never right."

The men sat there with their drinks and seemed to ponder it all to the bottom of those pint glasses. Another round came for them while they sat there, watching the TV absently. Kayla downed her two drinks and ordered another set. She got change and went to the jukebox, charged it up and set herself in a chair beside it while the speaker rattled her eardrum.

Half an hour passed and she saw the one talker move out from his stool and hike up his jeans. The man moved near underwater slow as he shuffled away from the bar and stood down to the floor proper. He turned and went through the pool-room, smacked a loose cue ball on the table so that it rifled around by the banks. There were a few people playing darts and he waved at them but they didn't see him or didn't care. Tall, barrel-chested man of about thirty with a great block of a head built right into his shoulders. For all that, he had a boy's face.

Kayla followed him along a dim corridor until he turned and started down a set of shortstairs. The washrooms were below. She came in close as he was navigating the first step and there she wound up and booted him in the ass. He went over like he'd been fired from a cannon and his arms tried for the walls but he didn't touch anything until he landed face and chest first to old carpet and concrete below and carried on ass over teakettle through a line of spent kegs. Kayla ducked low to better see the bathrooms. Nobody came out. He was moving around in the kegs with his face-down and legs pumping slow, like a dog shifting dirt by its head.

She went through to the bar and sat. Nobody looked at her. She felt like she'd just come back from the moon. The bartender got her one more set of drinks and she sipped the first. The man hadn't returned yet and his fellow at the bar was checking the clock on his phone. Kayla paid the bartender. Stood and slugged back the second drink. She thanked him and took up her jacket. She left.

KAYLA COULDN'T FIND A JOB AND SHE couldn't find a job. Her unemployment insurance was set to expire before summer's end and the rooming house ate most of what she had left in the bank. Matthew had come around somewhat and she'd been able to talk to him on the phone and visit him a few times a week. He'd lost more weight but he'd gained something back by his eyes. When she looked at him he was actually there.

On a Friday afternoon Kayla cleaned herself up and put on a dress and pinned her hair up. She parcelled books for Matthew to read and some candy bars for him to hide in his drawers. She had very little money she could give him. She drove to the hospital in the truck, the windows wound down. Hot, humid air and not a breeze but what she made by driving. Trash bins cooking streetside as they waited for their hauling. By the time she got there her hair had gone crazy and her dress stuck to the middle of her back. She parked and brushed at her hair by the rear-view mirror. After awhile she gave up and got out.

She signed in at the front desk and there he met her. They kissed small and by the sides of their lips like old people. Then they went outside with different coloured tags strung around their necks. Matthew's hands were shaky yet and while they walked the grounds of the hospital he was bowed over slightly and took his steps too slow.

"There's an awful lot of young people in here," she said.

"I know it."

"I was told they get a kick outta you."

He smiled crooked.

"I'm like the uncle that'll buy 'em beer."

"Yeah?"

"I'm telling ya. Some of them got stories that'll curl your hair."

Kayla nodded. She held his one hand in the both of hers as they went. There were few others out there with them on the grasses. Three old men sat smoking at a picnic table, the one a huge black man in an electric wheelchair, bag of breadcrumbs that he pitched out for the pigeons. A loose bird had alit to his knee and the man watched it close until it dropped again and went about its pecking.

"How are you?" Matthew said.

"I'm okay."

"What about the apartment?"

"It's fine," she said.

He studied her long.

They sat right in the grass and Kayla crossed her legs and pulled her dress over them. He reached under to her ankle and held it gentle. Let go. He leaned back on the grass by both arms and made a sound. Pulled up again and rolled his right shoulder a couple times. She asked him if it was okay and he said it was. They sat quiet for some time.

"Were those fellas alright in the end?" he said.

"What?"

"The ones that I got into it with that night. Those two men."

"Sure," Kayla said.

OUT BY THE CITY LIMITS SHE IDLED at a turnoff and held one hand up against the setting sun. There were a few other cars and they were all in the other turning lane. The light changed and she took her turn and drove on. Not long down that road she saw farm fields and wood fences. Houses planted sparely in their plots. Hundred year willows tickled the truck roof as she passed by. Kayla knew that she'd gone out of the county inside of three minutes and she slowed the truck and then almost right away put her foot back to the pedal.

She ate a burger from a grilltruck in a gravel lot, sitting at a nearby picnic table with its western legs sunk into the ground some. Fruit stand in the lot-corner met by passing tourists. The attendant didn't seem to mind the customers one bit, even to help them pay him. Bugs bit at Kayla's legs by the shorts-line.

Two ants cycled on her thigh and she watched them a second and then flicked them clear. From her dinner seat she saw thin smoke in the sky, followed it down to where it spun from the round chimneys of a great sheet metal building. Kayla took the last mouthfuls of her burger with her and left out.

THE SIGN READ ABOUT GOOD MEN needed and she stood there looking at it. She went back to the truck and climbed up to the benchseat. Unbuttoned her shorts and shuffled out of them. Went behind the seat for her pants. She put her hair back and walked the lot to the building's front doors.

There were men working the lines, inspecting sinkbasins. A few of the machines were being seen to by technicians with their toolbelts and soiled forearms. Almost all of them stopped a second to take a look at her before putting their heads back down to their work. Low, steady hum of ever-moving beltlines. Hiss and pop of pneumatic tools as they applied fasteners. Kayla found the site offices and moved along them until she saw the manager's nameplate. The door hung open and he was standing there with his hands on his hips, studying a wall-built corkboard. Stocky man of about fifty with almost pure grey hair, stubble at his chin. She knocked and he turned.

"What can I help you with, miss?" he said.

"I see you might be lookin' for good people."

"Your boyfriend got any experience in an outfit like this?"

"My husband."

"Your husband got any experience in an outfit like this?"

She smiled.

"He's in the hospital right now," she said.

The man turned back to the corkboard and shook his head.

"You lookin' for somethin' for him when he's well?"

"Maybe. But I'm well enough to work right now."

The man looked at her and out at the factory floor. He reached out his hand and Kayla shook it firm. He went to his desk and sat, waved a hand at a chair on the opposite side.

"Well, have a seat," he said.

So she did.

A WEEK IN AND SHE'D OCCUPIED a shaded swath of parking lot where she could stow the truck of a night. She ran a hundred-foot electrical cord to the truck from one of the chip wagon outlets and it powered her alarm clock and her phone charger and a small house fan that she laid on the floor sideways by the pedals. She found patches of screen at the hardware store with magnetted ends and fixed them to the window frames but she'd not lived in the country since she was young and after sundown there were either too many sounds or too few and she had to wind the windows up and lock the doors. Sleep didn't come easy and she had weird dreams in the shallows of it and often she dreamt of him.

Her second Thursday at work she punched out and ate chicken fingers in the lot, waited for the sun to go. Crickets had already begun their fiddling. At dusk she drove off, down the narrow county lane to a fieldroad walled in by cornstalks. She parked and walked the rows until she came to a wire fence. The field backed up against somebody's yard and in that yard they had an above-ground pool with the tarp drawn over it. Kayla forced the fencelines and went through. No dogs to declare her. She stripped to her skin and piled her clothes neatly by on a little wooden table. Went up the ladder with a bottle of shampoo in the one hand. She unhitched a corner of the tarp and folded it back. Over she went into the cool waters, let the bottle float the surface as she sunk down and sat on the container floor.

LONG AFTER DARK SHE WAS LAYING down in the truck with a tiny nightlight plugged into the power cable. It shone dimly from the passenger floormat. She'd drifted some and forgot to take the screens down. Out in the black there were warm winds travelling by and scenting the inside of the cab. Trace of skunkmist that twitched her nostrils. Whatever the trees and grasses and bracken let loose in the heat. She started to sleep again and then woke up full.

Somewhere in the lot there were feet dancing the gravel, a low throat-bound growl that had to be dog but she'd never heard its like. Kayla sat up to better see and regretted it right away. She could not see a goddamn thing through the screenwork but knew it in her guts that she could be seen clear by the meagre interior bulblight. She lay back down and pulled the light from the socket. She heard her heart like a kickdrum and thought up all the animals she'd come across or even just ever heard of.

She pushed the screen out on the passenger side and wound the window shut, turning the lever slow. Loud snuffling right there below the driver door. The truck shifted slight and she could just stare down at her feet and let her brain take it. Black nothing of the world outside the driver window and the odd scent of damp hair. Kayla had not made a sound but she'd tears at her cheeks and she tasted one where it trailed and then she'd had enough. The truck kept moving small on its suspension by whatever pushed at the sidepanels and she sat up and punched the screen clear. She wound the lever so hard that the knob bent on its screw. With the window pinned she dropped prone again and waited. The truck was still and it was still and then she felt it move but once. Kayla lifted a leg and put her bare heel to the horn and kept at it.

In the morning she came to work haggard and went right past her station to the boss' office. He had just about sat with his morning coffee and he stopped halfway and got back up.

"I hear you got a trailer for rent," she said.

He waved at the seat across his desk.

SHE DROVE THE HIGHWAYS TOWARD the city proper, on new tires and brake pads that she'd paid for outright. Kayla had put the pads on herself with the help of a hydraulic pumpjack from the factory. One of the fellas had talked her through it but she'd done the work. The bed of the truck had been cleared and cleaned. Tool containers mounted on the frame, below the back windows of the cab. Kayla had the windows down as she drove and her dress danced by her legs and her hair blew at her shoulders but she didn't mind. The county roads were thick with fallen leaves. The fields all about her had been harvested and tilled black. There were cool winds supposed to come early from somewhere out on the prairies. Not yet.

When she pulled into the visitor lot he was sitting there on a bench with a duffle bag full with his clothes. A box of his books and other necessaries sat on the pavestones by his feet. Kayla all but stopped breathing a minute and parked crooked in the spot. Her cheeks had gone red. She didn't know why. She got out of the truck, stood behind the open door and smoothed her dress against her legs. Matthew stood up full and slung the duffle over his shoulder, took the box up under one arm and walked the asphalt to meet her.

THEY DROVE A WINDING DIRT LANE to where the trailer sat. Half-naked tree branches stropped the sides of the vehicle as they went. Matthew had his forearm outside the passenger window and it took its lashings. Kayla studied him sidelong. He'd gotten a little fatter by the hips and through his neck and cheeks. He'd smiled more than once on the ride. She carried them on by the busted laneway until they reached the clearing.

Just packed clay for a front yard and the thin woods in back. Wildgrass aside the trailer and a dig-crater turned frogpond in the far west corner of the property. Matthew walked the site and puzzled over the cables that ran from the trailer to a thick wood post, industrial outlets built into the top part of it somehow. Kayla waited for him by the trailer steps. He came back eventually.

"We gonna be country folk?" he said.

"Looks that way."

He stood at the foot of the little stairwell and she was taller than him. Matthew put a palm to the trailer and gave it a shove. Nothing. The wheels were gone and it had long been pinned down and laid under with concrete blocks. He smiled and stood there.

"You did everything right," he said.

"Thanks," she said.

He came up the steps and put a hand to her hip. Kayla opened the door and let him go by. He had her by the belt and tugged. She went in behind him and let the screen door swing.

THERE IN THE HALF-LIGHT SHE could see him rolling about on the floor of the trailer. Legs cycling the air oddly and stopping. One leg going again. He might have been asleep and he might not have. She got out of the bed and set about getting her arms under him but she didn't. Instead she leaned back on her haunches and then sat ass-down on the floor herself and watched him dance. Matthew hadn't shook all of the old meds and they travelled his nerves yet and she didn't know what to do. Minutes in she edged over to him and got her hips to his belly, hooked the back of his knees with her heels and hugged his head and face. She held him there and soon he woke up. He hugged her down hard to him. Outside there were winds whipping the trailer boxmetal. They'd left the inner door open. Dank smell of animal hair again and it came and went. Wet leaves had blown flat to the middle part of the screen.

"Don't ever put me back in there again," he said.

"Okay," she said. "Just go to sleep."

ACKNOWLEDGEMENTS

THE STORIES IN THIS BOOK, and the book itself, would not have seen the light of day if not for the journals that took a chance on my work. I have to recognize *The Malahat Review*, *The Puritan*, *PRISM international*, *EVENT*, *Joyland*, *Shenandoah*, *The Walrus*, *This Magazine* and especially *The New Quarterly*, for publishing three of the stories in here. Without these brave editors and publishers I'm not sure where I'd be.

I've had some fine readers to keep me straight, and have met many writers who have supported the work ever since they met it. There are instructors who got me to write real, honest stories some years ago, such as A.F. Moritz and Lindsay Clarke. And there are writers like Tamas Dobozy, Kathryn Kuitenbrouwer, Craig Davidson, and John Irving, who have taken time away from their own work to read and champion some of mine. I owe them all plenty and I'll not forget it.

My writing career found footing through my experience with The Journey Prize, and the work done there by Anita Chong and McClelland & Stewart, and The Writers' Trust of Canada. Most of the writers I've mentioned were met through my inclusion in *The Journey Prize Anthology* and the resulting events. The staff of The Writers' Trust, especially Mandy Hopkins and Katrina Afonso, were very kind from the beginning and patient with me when I went from doing most of my writing alone in the middle of nowhere and having few ties to the literary community, to being immersed in all of it at once, and attending things where I had to wear ties. Further, I have been through some hard years to get to this book, and The Writers' Trust was always quick to lend support. Through James Davies and The Writers' Trust committee, I was able to get help from The Woodcock Fund, and this actually kept a roof over my head while I worked on these stories. The lives of writers are made easier by these folks and their kindness and hard work.

I have also received funding from the Ontario Arts Council and the Writers' Reserve Program, after recommendation by Biblioasis and Scrivener Press, for work on this book. This was much needed and I am extremely grateful for it.

I don't like to think where this book would be without John Metcalf, my editor, who read one of my stories in a sea of those he reads from journals all over the country, and called me and wrote me for the rest of them. His finding that story changed my life. Through John my writing got to Dan Wells and Biblioasis, and I quickly knew that I'd landed in exactly the right place with the right editor and the right publisher. John and Dan, and Biblioasis staff like Grant Munroe, Kate Hargreaves, and Chris Andrechek, have helped me build this book and made it the powerful looking little thing you have in your hands right now. I was starting to think there might be no editors or publishers like this anymore, with the guts to engage with difficult work like this and take the time to develop it. It turns out I ended up with some of the last ones out there, and I think on that everyday. I am a very fortunate man.

Most importantly, I have to thank my family, who have fought and bled with me for all the years of my life. My brother, Peter, who has been at my side through the worst and best of things, and who I would take a bullet for. My mother and my father, who made me into the person I am and gave me the fortitude to endure and keep at the work, to have no quit in me. It is no secret that all of the stories here draw from our lives, and my family has been generous enough to let me tell them without any inclination to withhold, even if some of it hurts to read and rattles the soul. I thank my Canadian family and my family in north England, those who are here and those that left us with their stories. Since I was very young there were things chronicled and told and retold that would beggar belief. But they happened, and they have informed my writing from the beginning. Not least, I've had friends over the past twenty years who've been through the wars with me and have kept me honest. They know who they are.

I dedicate this book to my brother, and my mother, and my beloved father, who fought hard to stay with us but has gone and is missed very much. Everything I know and that I am is because of the man he was, and that has worked its way into these stories, each and all.

PHOTO BY KATRINA AFONSO

KEVIN HARDCASTLE's stories have appeared in *Shenandoah*, *The Walrus*, *The New Quarterly*, *This Magazine*, *The Malahat Review*, *EVENT*, *PRISM International*, and *Joyland*. Hardcastle lives in Toronto.